MW00929181

 PRESS

ASIAN MEN BLACK WOMEN BOOKS

6 STORY COLLECTION
VOLUME 1

AMBW PRESS
ASIAN MEN BLACK WOMEN BOOKS

6 STORY COLLECTION
VOLUME 1

AUTHORS:
JADE MOON
LOVE JOURNEY
KAY LEE
ONYX BLACK

COPYRIGHT

DESCRIPTION

AMBW Press presents *Asian Men Black Women Books Volume 1* – a 6 story collection of romance novellas.

Titles Included:

ALWAYS BACK TO YOU

BREATHE AGAIN

DIRTY DIVORCE

ART OF FLOWERS

FOREVER AHEAD OF US

SAMARA

AMBW PRESS ASIAN MEN BLACK WOMEN BOOKS – VOLUME 1

ALWAYS BACK TO YOU

A SECOND CHANCE NOVELETTE

BY

JADA MOON

AMBW PRESS ASIAN MEN BLACK WOMEN BOOKS – VOLUME 1

CHAPTER 1

Savang treads carefully, mindful not to step on a potentially icy stone on the pavement because he really shouldn't fall now, considering he has his son perched upon his shoulders. Kayson is in a great mood – he has been all day. It's Jurnee's week to have their son, but Savang had asked to take Kayson to the zoo to see the penguins, and they'd had a great time. They had so much fun that Savang might have extended the 4pm deadline to 5pm and is now exceptionally late to drop him back off again, but he'd at least texted Jurnee to alert her so she wouldn't worry. He'd gotten an "ok" back, which was about the extent of their conversations these days. She never asks him anything, and he doesn't know how to tell her what he's feeling.

As best friends, having a child together but maintaining a platonic relationship had seemed a good plan. The pressure to start a family had begun to overwhelm both of them, and it had seemed the ideal solution to their shared dilemma. They were exceptional co-parents, and Kayson was the happiest child for miles. In his secret heart, Savang had always believed that he and Jurnee would be together forever. It had been a perfect promise of an inevitable forever. But that was before other people had made their way into their lives and separated them.

Now, with daylight fading quickly as he carries Kayson back to his mother, Savang feels like everything is falling apart around him. He wants to tell Jurnee how he feels like his apartment is closing in on him, how he broke up with his girlfriend Lily two months ago over breakfast like it was an afterthought and he felt not a single emotion other than relief, how the Christmas season is killing him because everyone, as per the spirit, is going on and on about family while his is in shambles. And then he'd rediscovered a gift he had wanted to give her back in early summer and had formed a plan, or a semblance of one at least: He is going to give her that gift and hope for the best, hope that when she sees it, she'll know how he feels, even if he hadn't had the courage to tell her back then.

His feet are heavy as he puts Kayson down from his shoulders, holding on to the paper bag with Jurnee's gift with one hand and to his son's with the other as he takes the gravel path to her house. It's beautiful and welcoming from the outside – red brick with window boxes for flowers in the summer, now decorated with a Santa and elves and reindeer and twinkling lights – and he thinks it must be lovely on the inside as well, although he has never gone further than the hallway. He lifts Kayson up easily so he can ring the doorbell and smiles as brightly as he can when Jurnee opens the door, backlit by the warm, homey glow from the hallway while the front porch light reflects in her kind, wise, depthless brown eyes. She has on a touch of makeup, just enough to enhance her raw beauty: smooth skin the color of milk chocolate, delicate cheekbones, full, expressive lips that he remembers as having a playful, enticing twist when she was trying, unsuccessfully, to be serious in the face of his antics – though over the past year those beautiful lips became resolute, quietly unforgiving. At least toward him. Maybe he saw them quiver slightly, very briefly, in the fraction of a second when she first opened the door. And maybe it's his own wishful thinking. But he clings to his hope so that he won't lose courage again.

"Hey," she says with a bright smile that is not for Savang and bends down to both hug Kayson and carry him inside from the December cold. She sets him down well into the hallway, giving Savang just enough room to follow if he wants. She neither encourages it, nor discourages it, but is happy to see Savang step inside and shut the door.

He looks almost vulnerable in his thigh-length, charcoal-colored wool coat. His jet-black hair is slightly disheveled from carrying Kayson on his shoulders. Yes, Jurnee watched from the living room window where she had been reading to distract herself from how late they were. His ivory skin is touched by the cold, especially his cheeks, but somehow this also makes him more masculine - a lone warrior in a hostile environment, stoic against adversity.

His dark eyes meet hers, and she looks away, but not quickly enough to stop herself from wondering if the color in his cheeks is from more than the freezing temperature.

She crouches before little Kayson, unzipping him out of his winter coat and tugging his arms out of the sleeves. "Did you see the penguins, honey?"

Kayson fusses as she gets him out of his shoes and gurgles something barely intelligible about the zoo and about "Daddy," and Jurnee encourages him with questions about what else he saw and what he ate for dinner, but only until he is finally out of his winter wear.

"Alright, listen, it's bedtime," she says more to Savang than to their son and stands up, moving her body towards Savang as if to push him out of her home. "We should say goodnight to your Dad. It's already past your bedtime."

Kayson starts complaining immediately, teetering on the edge of a terrible-two's-tantrum and repeats the word "no" while stomping his feet and then burying his face against his mother's legs, beating at them with his tiny fist. He's a little guy, but the force of his protest pushes her sideways a step, just enough so that her back isn't completely to Savang anymore.

"Wait," Savang says, trying to defuse the situation before she turns him out into the cold again. He rummages in his bag for the gift he'd brought.

"I know you have him on Christmas, and that's alright, but I have a gift for you, and I wanted to hand it to you in person."

"Oh, that's nice," Jurnee says, friendly but dismissive and unwilling to really meet his eye, let alone reach for the oblong package he is holding out to her. It looks hefty, wrapped in gold paper – the kind of paper one would expect to see a diamond necklace wrapped in. It also looks like a trap. "But I don't need a gift or anything, that's fine."

"No, please just take it," he pleads, bordering on desperation, which he is doing his best to hide. "You can throw it away if you don't like it."

"Open it, open it!" yells Kayson with excitement. He lets go of her leg to touch his chubby little palm to the wrapping paper and set out on the futile attempt of ripping it open himself.

"I don't…" Jurnee tries to form a coherent sentence, her ears feeling warm the way they had years ago when anyone had asked them if they were a couple or not, and Kayson cuts her off.

"Open it, Mommy!" he yells again, and Jurnee visibly squirms.

"No, baby," she tells their son and then lets him bawl on a bit before addressing Savang. She's angry. She's wary. she wants to lash out at him for using their son as a pawn for whatever his agenda is. Not that he did so intentionally – she realizes this – but why did he have to insist on giving her a gift now, after a long day, when her nerves were strung, and Kayson was beyond his two-and-a-half-year threshold for patience? But she's also bone-weary from a year of sharing parental responsibilities with a man who seemed utterly uninterested in her, the one man on Earth from whom this lack of interest could sting. Miraculously, she manages a mostly civil tone: "Thanks for taking him to the zoo. But I really need to put him down now. He's exhausted."

Before Savang can do or say anything to change her mind, his son comes through for him hard, screaming and stamping his feet: "Daddy, stay!"

He shakes his head a little at Jurnee and takes half a step back hesitantly. He doesn't want to go without having handed her the gift, but Jurnee looks so uncomfortable he would rather leave now, just to make her feel a bit happier.

But Kayson is out of control now, kicking and screaming. "Daddy, stay and open the present," he shrieks.

"Okay," Jurnee says. "We'll say goodbye to Daddy, and then I'll open the present. I'll open the present if you promise to go right to sleep after. But remember, after I open it, then you're going to bed."

"I want Daddy to tuck me in!" Kayson screams and finally uses his trump card, which is to throw himself on the floor and pound his fists on the hardwood floors.

"No, buddy," Savang tries, feeling sorry for having caused all this havoc, but his voice barely carries over his son's tantrum. He looks at Jurnee forlornly, trying to tell her he's sorry and that this isn't what he wanted, but she only holds his gaze for a moment before plucking a screaming Kayson from the ground and saying: "Okay, Kayson! We're going to both get you ready for bed and then we're going to open the present. Then you're going to go sleep, okay?"

"Okay?" Savang asks Jurnee, trying to make sure if this is really alright, but she just shrugs and hands him the thrashing boy who is appeased once he registers that he's gotten what he wanted.

Jurnee leads the way, walking ahead of Savang like he's an intruding stranger, and tells him she's sorry for the mess.

But it's not messy at all. There are two stray toys lying on the couch under the window, and a baby blue blanket draped over the back of one of the chairs. The rest is inviting, furniture-catalog ready: a thriving peace lily on a stand in one corner, a brass floor lamp in the other corner, a cherry wood coffee table in front of the couch, with a half-finished cup of tea next to a paperback novel, bookmark carefully wedged between the pages halfway through the book.

Savang takes a moment to close his eyes and inhale deeply. He has a hard time coping with the scent of the place because it's all Jurnee. Like home. Vanilla and strawberry and sweetness, and he wants to cower in a corner or rub his face on the carpet, inhaling her fragrance that permeates the place. If he could bottle up this aroma and take it with him, it would soothe him wherever he goes, but it would also torment him. A delicious yet painful reminder that he is no longer a meaningful part of her life, and she no longer part of his.

She leads them upstairs, turns the corner, and there is Kayson's room. It looks like the room he'd had back when they were all living together, the same light blue color scheme, the same dresser, toy chest, and rocking chair – just a bigger bed now that Kayson is getting so grown-up. Above his changing table with the baby powder and a neat stack of diapers, on a shelf with stuffed lions and bears and a baby monitor, still in use because Jurnee is still protective of her little man, hangs Kayson's name tag from the hospital.

"So, let's get you in your pajamas, and then we'll open the present, alright?" Jurnee asks Kayson, and Savang tries to make himself useful. He is confused by the way she has sorted his clothes, but he finds the pajamas on the second attempt. He picks a pair that he liked from when Kayson's revolving wardrobe had brought some clothes to the dresser at his place. He finds that the pajamas don't fit well anymore. But Jurnee accepts them anyway.

"You're getting big, huh?" Jurnee asks her son, trying to maneuver him into the shirt.

"I big," Kayson says proudly, throwing his arms in the air to show them how big he is, and Savang's eyes are suddenly damp with tears.

"Here, let me do it," he offers and tries to coax Kayson's little arm through the small sleeve.

"Thanks," Jurnee says, staunchly not looking at him, but together, they manage to get their son into his pajamas and onto his bed, where they wedge him between them both and place the present on his small lap.

"Do you want to open it?" Jurnee asks him with a smile, but Kayson shakes his head.

"No, Mommy. You open it," he says with the exaggerated enthusiasm only a two-and-a-half-year-old can do adorably, and so she does. She tears away the layers of gift-wrap until she hits the box. She lifts the lid and drops it to the side, and then starts peeling back the gauzy white crepe paper.

"What is that?" she asks Kayson playfully. "What could that be?"

When she finally pulls the gift free of the crepe paper, she pauses. She looks at the book Savang has made for her, thick leather cover with no title, pages overflowing with the lifetime of memories they have together.

Kayson's little fingers shoot out to the cover of the book. Feeling like she has no control over her voice or her words, she feigns cheerfulness when she asks Kayson, "So you want to open it?" She keeps her eyes carefully off of Savang. Her spine feels like it is made of shattered ice, and every move she makes comes from someone else's will. Maybe Savang's. Maybe Kayson's. She balances the book on her left thigh – the book is wide enough that it would bury Kayson's little legs – and helps Kayson to open it.

The first page is a punch to the gut, a title page with their names together, written out in Jurnee's elegantly scrolling calligraphy. Beneath it is a faded photo of two kids playing on the swings, reaching out to each other, faces lit with laughter. This book is a project they had started years ago, during the summer when Jurnee had taken a week-long calligraphy-writing course. The force of the memory is so vivid. She can smell the Lao coconut cake cookies that Savang's mom had been baking as Jurnee and Savang leaned over their stack of pictures. She purposefully hadn't looked at these photos since their falling out, and for a good reason.

"Do you know who that is?" Savang asks Kayson, resting his fingers below their pictures, his hand close enough to Jurnee's that she could feel its warmth.

"Mommy and Daddy," says Kayson.

"You're right, that's Mommy and Daddy," Savang tells him softly, and Jurnee throat closes up slowly.

"A long time ago," she adds and quickly flips through the next several pages, past Halloween photos, homecoming, and their prom.

"Look, Kayson, this is you," Savang says, pointing at a candid picture of Jurnee at their friend April's wedding, Jurnee with daisies in her thick straight black hair and her big round baby belly at seven months. She was so crazed for his touch back then that she was glowing every time he was near, and that's so painfully captured for all eternity in this picture. It's strange how happy she looks, how dazed and in love, even if she hadn't known she was back then or hadn't admitted it to herself at least. She remembers that Savang had plucked the daisies from April's bouquet, an uncharacteristically exuberant gesture on his part.

It occurs to her that this may have been the beginning of the end for them before Kayson was even born. April was the first of their friends to get married. Meanwhile, Jurnee's status remained officially "single."

"This is you inside Mommy's tummy," she tells her son over a grin that is hard to maintain. She feels it wavering and, to disguise her true emotions, says with forced enthusiasm, "Look how big I was, like a balloon!"

"You looked beautiful, that's my favorite picture," Savang tells her, and she can feel his eyes on her, knows the crinkle of his eyes by heart, and knows how his lips open, how he licks them, how he studies her, without having to look. Just his proximity tonight is stirring those emotions that never completely go away, emotions that, when muted, she believes she could live with, but now that they are starting to awaken within her, she realizes she had forgotten how powerful they are.

"Alright, that's enough," she says and snaps the book closed before she breaks down. She swoops up, Kayson right behind her, making Savang leap off the bed. "Let's put you to bed, honey, we had a deal."

Kayson is pliant enough and lets her put him under the covers. She gives him a long kiss on the forehead that she uses to steady herself and hopefully hold on to what little composure she has left. Then she steps back to let Savang say goodnight to him too. Savang is leaning down to give him a kiss when Kayson's little voice starts mumbling.

"I want Daddy to sleep at our house," he says, and the world ends.

Savang turns around to look at Jurnee, looking up with panic written on his face, and she can't do much but stare back at him in horror. They are not ready to have this conversation.

"Honey," she starts, but it seems Kayson is not done tearing her heart open.

"Why doesn't Daddy sleep at our house?" he asks.

"Well." She tries bending down to be closer to him, hoping that by the time she knows what to say, she'll still have a voice. "Daddy sleeps at his house, and you know what?"

"Why?" Kayson says, eyes big, waiting for a grown-up piece of wisdom that Jurnee has to scramble to produce.

"That's why you have two houses to sleep in because you're the most special boy in the world and only really special kids get two houses to sleep in," she rambles, hoping her son will be satisfied with her explanation.

Unfortunately, she will never find out because then Savang, crouching by the bed, makes a monumental mistake.

"I wish I could sleep at your house, buddy," he says, and Jurnee lets out a hiss. He turns around to meet her gaze, and she looks like she could end him right there on the spot. Just not in front of their child.

"What are you doing?" she asks him under her breath, and he just shrugs at her.

"I want to stay at your house," he repeats shamelessly, looking at her with his dark eyes wide and innocent and hopeless, and she could strangle him with her own two hands.

But instead, she turns back to Kayson, pats his blanket a couple of times and says: "Okay, sweetie, I love you so much. Goodnight."

With that, she snaps back up and leaves the room, hissing at to Savang on her way into the hallway and shutting off the lamp, leaving him to say goodnight to his son in the dim glow of his nightlight.

By the time he leaves Kayson's room and closes the door behind him, Jurnee has already paced a hole into the carpet. She cuffs his shoulder when he's close enough to reach. It's like lashing out at a dejected, injured puppy, unsatisfying, but she realizes her sympathy for him is the only thing keeping her from pushing him down the stairs. She also realizes she hates the hungry, lost look in his exotic eyes, the strained pinch in his cheeks, the way his lips look like he hasn't smiled in years. With a word, a gesture, she could change all that, restore the twinkle in his eyes, smooth the frown from his clear, ivory forehead. As if she is the reason for his misery.

Realizing this rekindles her anger. "What was that?" she asks him, keeping her voice low enough so Kayson wouldn't hear. "Do you want to tell me what that was about?"

"I'm sorry," is all he says. Now it is his turn to not meet her gaze.

"Sure you are," she snaps, then catches herself, taking a deep breath, not wanting to hurt him more than he is already. "You can't say things like that," she tells him, more calmly. "Not in front of Kayson." And never in front of me, she wants to add, but doesn't.

"I know," Savang says hurriedly and sheepish. "I know, and I'm sorry. I didn't want him to think that..."

"Think what?" she challenges. "Think what, Savang?"

Instead of answering, he jumps at her, hands first closing behind her neck with his fingers in her hair, and then crashes his lips onto hers. The violence of his need makes her head spin, momentarily. Her heart thuds heavily and then drops to the floor.

"Don't do that," she says, pushing him away. "Please. Don't do that." Instant heat seeping thawing the chill in her heart.

"I'm sorry," he says again. He's almost as shocked as she is.

"Look, I'm sorry if you're lonely, Savang, I'm sorry your mother calls me every other week to tell me how guilty you feel, but I can't do this with you again. You can't have it both ways. You absolutely can't come into my house and say all these confusing things to a two-and-a-half-year-old, you just can't. You're the one who wanted to move on. You're the one who left us. The one who left me. I had to pick up the pieces."

"I know," he says. Savang just can't stop staring at her. Jurnee can't believe that this is happening and that she still wishes it could be real despite her better judgment.

"You keep saying that. 'You know.' What do you know? That you hurt me? I'm past that. I'm finally in a good place," she says. It's a lie, but it's getting truer by the day. "I'm not angry with you. I'm not pining for you. I'm keeping busy. I'm doing good. So just go home, Savang. You don't need to do this."

"Jurnee," he tries.

"No," she cuts him off, "Please, whatever it is. Don't do this to me. Just leave. Please."

And so he does, even if he takes his time and stops twice on the steps down, bracing himself against the wall.

She believes he is sincere, that he's not exaggerating. It's not like him to permit himself to appear so vulnerable. The change from earlier, when she thought of him as a stoic warrior, alone in a hostile environment, alarms her. Even more alarming: it sends a shivery stab of sympathy through her heart. It occurs to her that he is a strange mirror, reflecting her innermost feelings. His strength just before he risked driving her further away with his gift is the same as her strength, every day, forging her way through life without him. His utter dejection now is also the same as hers. The final time he stops, she silently calls for him to come back.

But he is the one leaving – again – which is why she doesn't vocalize her feelings. He's the only one who can fix this. And he doesn't turn around because whatever he feels for her, it's not enough to stay and make his case, obviously.

When the door closes, she sits on the landing and hugs her knees to her chest, allowing herself five minutes to run through the gauntlet of emotions, hoping that this hasn't just thrown her back eight months. It is a familiar trek: first guilt, then anger at herself for feeling guilty.

Why should she feel guilty about protecting herself? Then her anger at him flares again, with a new twist: anger for his reckless antics in there with Kayson that will paint her as the villain in their child's eyes, as the one who doesn't want Daddy to sleep in their house.

And another new twist: the way he reached for her and kissed her, like he can just have her whenever he wants, like she's a piece of furniture, a book he flips through at his leisure and then never puts back on the shelf, just leaving her there, open on the floor. Whatever he feels is enough to embolden him, momentarily. But it's not enough to fight for her, for once in his life.

Then her five minutes of anger and self-pity and – she hates to admit this – hope is up. She tries to stuff the blizzard of raw emotions back into the box where it belongs, gets up, and starts getting ready for bed. It's six o'clock on a Saturday evening, but oh well. This is what her life is now.

Savang drives off, on autopilot, dimly aware of the moon rising behind the bare tree branches, but it is an awareness that means nothing. He is numb to everything around him. The chill in the air can't touch him – he is gripped by something colder than all the Decembers of his life combined. He feels like he is driving on ice, slowly sliding away from where he needs to be with no power to stop. He may as well expect to touch the face of the moon by reaching for it. Will it be like this forever, Jurnee always seemingly so near, glowing with an intense love that freezes when she looks at him? Is he being selfish to think he should ever have this from her again?

But the torment of picking up Kayson and dropping him off every week, all the while knowing he would never have another chance with Jurnee again. He doesn't think he can bear this. His memories of what they had together are too strong. To have seen her warm, soft eyes smile at him with love, and to now see cool indifference when she looks at him, makes him keenly feel that he is a sickness, an ugliness and that he will inevitably destroy everything he cares for. Maybe, to protect himself from how he feels, he should cry off, grant full custody to Jurnee so that he never has to endure her gaze and how it makes him feel about himself, surrender to his lonely fate, and hope he can eventually move on.

The thought causes bile to rise in his throat. How despicable he would be to abandon Kayson, to hurt him with what would look like another rejection when Kayson is too young to understand. It would be a repetition of the same mistake. Hasn't he learned his lesson yet?

And just as bad, the thought of never seeing Jurnee again, of never seeing the way she tilts back her head when she laughs, or her eyes half-closed with pure delight – even if he can only be part of this from a distance – sends chills through his spine. Kayson is their son, his as much as hers, and so when she hugs Kayson or kisses his tears away, she is also hugging and kissing Savang by proxy, no matter how she avoids looking at him.

Savang can't let go of this. He closes his fists around the steering wheel, realizing he had driven only a few blocks before stopping at an intersection. The light turns green, and drivers behind him start honking. Perhaps they have been honking for some time already. He doesn't know. But he must make a decision, now, once and for all.

As the light turns yellow, he signals to make a U-turn, his heart pounding, his stomach in knots, still uncertain but gathering his resolve. Even though it should be too late – the light is now red – he turns back.

Back at Jurnee's house, he nearly runs into the door, beating his fist against it and ringing the bell up a storm. When she finally opens the door for him, she's in her favorite sweatpants and an old t-shirt, faded red with a radio station logo cracked and peeling on the front. He realizes it's one of his t-shirts from years ago, the t-shirt he was wearing the first time he spent the night with her. He wonders if she remembers the shirt's history, but even if she doesn't, he has to take this as a good sign. He has to, or he will lose the courage to go on. Her face above the t-shirt looks flustered, exhausted. She's taken off her make-up, her skin still moist from the cleansers, her cheekbones shiny with natural, raw beauty. Loose strands of hair frame her face. Her eyes are wide and defenseless. She takes his breath away – literally. He can't breathe while standing on her porch. There just isn't enough air for him outside.

"Savang?" she just says as he pushes past her into her hallway.

"I can't just leave," he tells her.

"Savang, please..."

"No," he cuts in. "Please just let me say it. Let me say it, just once."

Jurnee groans, a mix of emotions flying through her so fast she can barely process them. She can do nothing but shrug, and it's as much permission as he's going to get, so he takes a deep breath, plucks all the courage he's ever had, and starts to speak.

"I love you." It's a good start, he thinks. "I was wrong to leave you. I was scared, Jurnee, terrified. This is so much bigger than me." He gestures between the two of them, hoping she'll understand. "The scope of my feelings for you, it just crashed down on me that day, and I couldn't handle it. I could handle pining for you and wanting you – I thought I could, at least – but when there suddenly was that possibility that we could finally be together, I shut down. I ran away. I'm so sorry. I've been sorry from the moment it happened. I haven't lived, not a day, since."

Jurnee doesn't respond, she just stays where she is and looks at him, and he does the only thing he can think of: he sinks down to his knees and begs her. "Please. I know I hurt you, I know you have no reason to forgive me."

And that is when his voice breaks and the tears begin to flow. "But I need you to know. I need you to know that I died a little bit every day, hating myself. Jurnee, I know how this sounds, but I'm not doing this because I'm lonely, or I'm feeling guilty, but because this is not much of a life I'm living anymore. I can't feel myself without you. I don't know who I am. I think about you every waking moment, and I want you so much, it's tearing me apart. And I ruined it, I did. I destroyed us, and we got this whole thing backward. I should've known I would mess it up, but here I am. I'm broken without you. I won't put it upon you to fix me. I'll walk right out of here if you say the word, but I can't go back to my life and not say this. Please give me another chance to finally get it right. I know I don't deserve it. I never wanted to hurt you, Jurnee. I just hurt myself so much more than you could ever imagine. I love you. I love everything about you, and in every conceivable way. I love you. That's what it comes down to. I love you."

He stops and looks up, gazing up at the love of his life as if she's the stars and the moon. Her eyes are brimming with tears, and there's an expression on her face that he's never seen in all his years knowing and loving her.

"Damn it," she says.

He's terrified again. He's used to it, so it just falls to the wayside.

"Damn it." She goes on. "What am I supposed to do with that?" She gestures at him, crouching on the floor before her, and he can't help but reach up and put his hands on her hips, holding onto her for dear life. She takes it in her stride. "You just barge in here and say all these things, and I'm supposed to just believe you and forget everything that happened? Everything you've put me through?"

"I know what I've said and what I did, and I know you won't believe me, but I never wanted to do that, I have no idea still why I left either, but all I can say is, it was just too much. I wasn't ready. I know this isn't the best time, and we've hurt each other a lot along the way, but you're the love of my life, Jurnee. You're my person. You're everything, and you have been for as long as I can remember. I miss you so much."

He finds her hands pressed to her side, finds them and tugs. "I miss you every day." He tugs. And finally, she sinks down to the floor to him, ending up face to face, closer than they have been in months.

Her eyes are wild and unreadable, but he finally lets her see him again, holds that connection to her, and strips himself naked of all his armor, letting her see that he is serious, that this is all that ever mattered, all that will ever matter again.

"Don't you miss me? Even a little?" He tries a desperate last resort.

"I miss you a little," she whispers, finally, and Savang's heartbeat is so erratic, he almost misses her voice over the rush of blood past his ears. "But I'm scared, Savang. I'm scared that you'll just change your mind again."

Instead of rambling on again, he closes the distance between them and kisses her, hard and pleading, and this time, she lets him. This time, she gives some of her own pressure back as her palm settles on his neck, the other one clutching his coat, pulling him in gently, tentatively. She makes a sound against his mouth, and he doesn't know if it is a soft protest or barely checked eagerness or a mix of both and everything in between, but she continues. He could get lost in this, in the silkiness of her cheek against his, the tickle of her fluttering eyelashes, the satin of her lips, and the warmth of her mouth, but she's spoken from her heart, and he needs to address it.

"I won't change my mind," he breaks away to tell her, holding her inches away from his face so he can speak. "This is it for me, and you're it. It's always been you. I was just too stupid and blind and scared to acknowledge it, Jurnee. I'll never fall out of love with you. I never stopped loving you, and I never will stop loving you. I don't think I even know how. Loving you is who I am."

He kisses her again, softer this time and shorter before he's leaning out again. "Please," he begs, once more. "Please give me one last chance. Please. Let me make love to you."

She looks at him for an eternity in a moment, and there is that flicker of a smile crossing her lips that makes him dare to hope. "Then," Jurnee starts, and he doesn't breathe. "Make love to me."

It's all he needs.

Jurnee's body is liquid. It's a good thing Savang takes the lead where they're sitting in her hallway, and he scoops her up into his arms, lifting her from the ground easily until she is propped on his hips, held up by one of his arms while the other navigates them through her house, around the corner to the guest room she points out him to dimly. She knows that this will take a while to process, but what she is absolutely certain of, is that she wants this with all her heart.

"Jurnee," he says and seems to not have much of a reason for it other than wanting to say her name as they reach the guest bedroom, and he gently puts her down on the floor, kicking the door closed behind him. She looks at him in the bluish sheen of the moonlight coming in from the blind, turning the darkroom blue, and traces his face with her fingertips. He smiles that bright smile she hasn't seen him smile in a while, and it reminds her of so many wonderful moments with him, so much happiness and so much love. He kisses her again, and when he leans over, his face has switched back to that smoldering intensity, the one that is hers alone and snakes his hands under her shirt, and then he slowly strips her out of it.

She's bare underneath and gasps when his hands brush her nipples, and he draws in a sharp breath.

"You're so beautiful," he whispers reverently, and undoes the knot of her pajama pants, kissing the corner of her mouth and then trails little kisses and licks down her neck and shoulder, her arm and the side of her body, turns her while doing it, so her legs hit the bed behind her. She sits down so he can finish rolling the pants off of her. He kneels in front of her again, and she's naked as the first day they made love while he is still fully clothed, and he barely gets his winter coat off before he puts his mouth on her.

"I've missed this so much," he says into her flesh, or at least that's what she thinks he says.

She has forgotten how his nose bumps against that particular spot when he does that. She's also forgotten how quickly that alone sends her spiraling out of control. She recalls the way he uses his tongue to flick and test around, and before long, she can't decipher what exactly he does down there, knowing only that it's warm and soft. He grabs her left leg by the ankle and props it on his shoulder, leaning in more, with his free hand pulling her against his face by the hip. Bonelessly, Jurnee arches into him, her hand falling onto his head to grab his hair and reinforce the faster pace he starts going for now.

She pants and moans and thinks letting him do this to her might be the best decision she has made in a while. Touching herself these past months hasn't even come close to how it feels when he does, and she wonders how she even survived this long without him, how she survived her own life. How she has almost forgotten the way, he could make her feel – like the universe is collapsing in on itself, and he is at the center of it all.

He hums and growls in turn, making her walls vibrate with the sound.

"Savang," she winces her approval and bucks into his face desperately. He laughs, muffled by her skin, and works his tongue into her with skill and experience. "Oh, god."

He withdraws his hand from her ankle, spreading her open, finding every last spot he hasn't lavished with attention yet while his fingers dance over her like he has a treasure map, and he knows exactly where to go.

"Savang, I'm going to..." she trails off, almost already over the edge.

He murmurs her name against her and leans in for one last caress, lips, tongue, and fingers going in, and she peaks, engulfed in flames, with a whimper, shakes violently, and comes back to life with a scream, split open as she cries out. While she's coming, he keeps at it, slightly twisting his wrist, getting a different angle both inside her trembling heat and on her twitching skin, so that it lasts even longer, doubles in on itself and her eyes roll back into her skull like she just might pass out.

Dimly, through the hard orgasm that is slow to wear off, she feels him pull his fingers out past her body's very own resistance. It's not conscious, but she's clutching him there all the same. He looks deeply content, a smile playing at his lips, eyes partially closed to soak in her pleasure with all his senses, the fact that he got her off giving enough indication that he's in it for the long run tonight and she knows he won't let her return the favor for a while. He wants this to last. To say she is delighted wouldn't cover half of it.

This is real, she thinks, finally. It's pure. It's them, together and in love. It's really all that matters.

She finds his eyes now, still kneeling before her, and he smoothes over the skin of her legs with lazy hands, kissing the inside of her thigh soft like a feather's graze, and she's all set to keep going. Just like that. He must know it because he flashes a wide, confident smile.

Her smile.

"That was," she starts but has to catch her breath to go on, "a good start." While her heartbeat booms through her, both of them know 'good' is a crass understatement.

"Yeah?" he asks anyway, a little desperate for her approval, and his eyebrows are tilting to which she responds with gentle pressure of her foot on his shoulder, softly kicking him away.

"Now, will you take those clothes off or what?" she says, bending forward to touch him, but he jumps to his feet, getting out of reach.

If he wants to play it like that, she's ready. She steps up to him, her feet protesting under the sudden shift of weight, but she remains stubborn and lifts her hands to his collar. He watches her quietly, shaking as she unbuttons his shirt, and his breathing is shallow, dotted with interruptions, and his hands are balled into fists at his side. Once she's got them all loose, it takes a bit of effort to roll the stiff fabric off his arms, especially because she tries to touch as much skin as she can before she gets it off and discards it to the floor. His white undershirt is next, and he gasps and shudders when she gathers it from under his belt and pants. She catches his eye just before she pulls it off of his head.

He interrupts her slow undressing of him by wrapping his glorious arms around her once more, and any faint taste of herself she might've found on his lips is gone when she kisses him. He pushes his tongue into her mouth, and she revels in his urgency. Apart from this, he remains still, just taking it in, getting used to being touched like this. He is still kissing her when she starts to fiddle with his belt buckle because she is getting antsy. Heat runs from her head into every single extremity and pools between her legs, shooting down. There's an ache deep within her where she suddenly feels empty without him.

"Impatient?" He chuckles against her lips and moves on to sweep his tongue along her jaw, nibbling and sucking wherever he feels like lingering. She has a good idea that he has been waiting for this moment. And so does she, so had she, she realizes, for the better part of her life.

"Bite me," she teases and has arrived at his button and zipper. It's a testament to her own self-control that she doesn't rip it open.

"I can do that," he says when she pushes down his pants. Glancing down between their bodies, she shivers with anticipation, while he is occupied sucking and biting the skin beneath her left earlobe raw, his faint stubble sure to leave her with beard burn and likely bruising from his mouth. His boxer briefs are going to be a bit harder to get off, stretched as they are over his length. She tries to be confident about it, but trembles for nerves and he gives a stifled hiss of pain when she yanks too hard, and his dick bounces free almost spitefully.

"Sorry," she says, "I'll make it up to you."

As the first muscle responds to her brain's commands, he's already stopped her, hands gripping her waist and neck as he steps out of his underwear.

"No," he says and kisses her cheek gently, finding her eyes after, and his features are soft and adoring and so much the man she has missed so much in the last year. She almost weeps. "I won't last if you do that."

"We've got time," she says, still a little impatient. She wants him in her mouth, and she doesn't mind one bit if he comes.

"Exactly," he says and then returns to his earlier spot beneath her ear to whisper. "I want to be inside you the first time." Her breath stalls.

She can live with that order of events just as well, and she means to tell him as much, all sultry, but the only thing she gets out is a shaky hum of assent. He hums in reply, smiling, and then she's suspended in the air again, wrapped around him, and he puts her on the bed gently, sighing in her ear. Then he kisses her, bent at an awkward angle above, for what feels like hours, and she thinks she might explode if he doesn't do something soon.

"You said something about coming inside me?" she reminds him, and he snorts out a laugh but then switches right back to sin as he lowers himself down onto her, arms propping him up on either side of her body. "Savang," she whispers. "Make love to me."

He gazes at her and watches, taking her in as he finally pushes inside without ceremony, filling her up, so she feels whole and complete beneath him, the last year and all the pain succumbing to this one moment of truth and she has a hard time keeping up with him when he starts moving from how overwhelming it all is.

She moans long and low, and he echoes her, his mewls, grunts, and gasps falling freely from his throat, louder every time she grinds her hips up to meet his thrusts.

After a while and some artfully executed position changes that leave both of them panting and sweating, he picks up the pace the way he does when he gets close, and he hasn't been lying about being too riled up to last very long. She can feel him tremble before he probably knows he's done with himself, and so he looks almost startled when he comes apart, eyes locked on hers, and she counts herself lucky that she gets to see his face do that again. She loves that she gets to see his mouth twitch and then stretch into that soundless "oh" and his eyes bulge as if his brain just burst. He jerks into her forcefully, two, three more times before he collapses on her mouth, kissing her with clumsy desperation like only she can give him back his peace of mind. He rolls his hips into her slowly after, at a leisurely pace, until the last wave of pleasure ebbs, and then he pulls out, keeping his lips on her body.

"I'm sorry," he whispers because he didn't wait for her to finish, but she doesn't mind.

"We have time," she tells him again and watches his flushed face turn to a grin.

"The rest of our lives," he says.

And just like that, at this very moment, it has all been worth it.

THE END

Breathe Again

AMBW Romance Novelette

AMBW PRESS
ASIAN MEN BLACK WOMEN BOOKS

BREATHE AGAIN

AMBW ROMANCE NOVELETTE

WRITTEN BY

ONYX BLACK

CHAPTER 1

The waitress was a slim, curvy brunette whose smile never faltered the entire night. It had a hopeful lilt, matched with eyes that simmered with lust. In return, Kris sent her a dry expression while Chen struggled to keep a straight face from mocking his brother.

"Can I interest you in some dessert?" She spoke to both but at the last word, stared at Kris.

"Just coffee, please," Chen answered when Kris looked away from her, hiding his annoyance. The girl huffed for the first time in the evening, realizing that the more handsome brother was not interested in her at all. She muttered something about checking on their order and walked away.

"So she does walk normally," Kris retorted, turning back and grunting under his breath. "I thought those hips were going to pop off with the way she was swaying."

"Be nice," Chen told him. "She can't help putting the moves on you. Despite being an idiot, you're the better looking of the two of us."

Kris snorted and brought a glass of water to his lips. "Not my type."

Though he had been taking a break from the entertainment industry, Kris could still be described as a heartthrob. His large exotic eyes that dramatically dipped at the outer corners were his most striking feature, or at least that's what his fans wrote on social media. He was taller than most at six feet and athletically built from all his years of training. He'd learned over the years that there was nothing like a sexy wink and a six-pack to make the girls go wild. He'd done it all. For years, he'd given his blood, sweat, and tears to the C-Pop boy band industry as a member of XXO - acting, singing, dancing, modeling, and eventually earned his own solo debut as one of the first English speaking Chinese hip hop artist from his label. He'd always loved music, but particularly hip hop and R&B. So he jumped at the chance to share his artistic soulfulness with the world.

Life had been good until he tripped and fell into the unforgiving grip of alcoholism. Years of alcohol abuse and neglect had ended in a sixteen-month long stint in rehab along with a scandalous reputation. The luring brown liquid had stolen his life and his career, but he was one of the lucky few. For Kris, rehab brought about healing and a chance at redemption. Everyone didn't get that opportunity. He felt lucky to have escaped death's grip so many times, and now he was determined to earn life back.

Chen rolled his eyes. "Unbelievable. Since we've sat down, a redhead model, whom I heard isn't particularly choosy with who she has sex with, made eyes with you until she left with someone else, a blond who actually had the guts to send you a drink inviting you to join her at the bar, and probably the most beautiful woman of the night, with a downright sexy British accent came right up to us, at this table," he tapped it with his finger for emphasis, "and said she would do me if you'd do her. And now that waitress who looks like she will be amenable to anything in bed. What are you waiting for?"

"I don't believe my manager would approve of my having an affair with a strange woman I picked up at a bar when she's working day and night trying to get me back on top of the billboard charts," Kris drawled. He continued to stare at Chen, who smiled at the frowning brunette when she returned but was ignored.

She served them their coffee, parroted the standard, "Enjoy your coffee," and put on a fake, painful smile then left. Kris let out an impatient sigh while Chen chuckled.

"Oh, I never thought I'd see the day when Arianna Holiday quite literally has a hold on you. And you've sunken as low as to move in with her and her boyfriend instead of coming home to your family after rehab?" he said. "I wonder what your ex-wife would say about that."

Kris shot him a warning glance before putting cream in his coffee. "Wow. You sure know how to ruin the night."

"I thought you would have dragged that woman through every court in the land," Chen said, ignoring his temper. "Forget it. She's not worth another thought. You know that."

"She's still family."

"More yours than mine."

Kris sighed. "I'm here tonight to prove to you that I'm still alive. Not to talk about my ex-wife."

"Fine. Fine. If I can't ask about Pamela, then let's go back to Arianna. Since when did your manager have a say about who you sleep with?"

Chen's favorite jokes involved sex, and there was no better audience for it than his equally raunchy brother. Kris could dish it back, but tonight, though it wasn't Chen's intent, he couldn't. Not when he was imagining Arianna panting in his ear, her beautiful hands eagerly guiding him into her. He twitched, imagining her hard thighs pinning him down, totally enslaving him with her beautiful eyes and her nipple piercings.

Quite by accident, he'd walked by as she was finishing a quick skinny dip in the hot tub the previous evening. He couldn't get over the image of her nipples looking chocolate and swollen, gleaming with the piercings, from the water.

His fascination with Arianna had been going on for as long as he could remember. She had the creamiest brown skin, hardly ever wore makeup, and often sported a serious expression on her face. But her eyes told a different story. The woman had the most striking hazel gold eyes he'd ever seen. Her eyes seemed to glow against her complexion, and they were framed by long thick eyelashes. He often got lost looking into them. Unfortunately, she used to be the most unpleasant company, as their manager, since she was always herding him and his old XXO band members like cattle and imposing limits to their fun. Like most young men that just wanted to have fun, they all rebelled when she put them on a schedule - up at the crack of dawn for a workout, a strict diet that only allowed one meal for indulgence, practices, and one rehearsal after another. She was tough as nails but delivered good results.

When she wasn't playing the management role, she really was a good, trusted friend, if not an important ally. Aware of her influence as the manager of one of the most famous Chinese R&B groups at the time, she'd gone on to donate as much as the group could spare to charities, single-handedly funding children's homes in most their home states.

Kris hated the fact that he had to go away for a year to finish his rehab and lose her to another man in order to realize he loved her. Not just an infatuation, but he was truly, madly, and deeply in love with this woman So much that her happiness was all that mattered to him.

When she told him the year before that she was engaged, Kris was devastated. His ex-wife was left, and he was alone. Now the one light in his life was gone, lost to a man that was unworthy of her. Kris couldn't bring him to like Xavier because he thought public relations guys were shallow, but in the days following her announcement, he realized he was going to have to accept the other man in her life or lose her completely.

Well, he tried but just couldn't force it.

After losing everything, when he realized that nothing was holding nor keeping him anymore, no XXO, no

Arianna, no nothing, he reached the point where he was ready to make a change in his life. He checked into the Progress Rehabilitation Center to reclaim his life from his addiction, deal with Pamela's ghosts, but most of all, to forget about loving Arianna. He knew that he was powerless over alcohol, and his life had become unmanageable. Therefore, he vowed never to touch the stuff again. And by the time left, Pamela was a distant memory. But Arianna was another story.

Again, he tried. He really did, but he just couldn't let go. Some of her was better than none of her.

He wasn't sure how he ended up in this situation, but now he was living with her, where she shared her bed with that other man. But he believed that a higher power was working in his life, and he needed to be near her to restore his sanity. Though sometimes he was haunted by the idea that Xavier would claim the love of his life, and Kris thought about disappearing to an island somewhere in the Pacific. It was just a thought. Instead, his solution became an investment in super silent heavy-duty earphones for the nights they would have sex. He dreaded sleeping at night, snapping awake every time he heard a groan or a squeak from the mattress next door. He heard nothing. Still, he wasn't in the house all the time. Who was to say they didn't sneak back in and have sex on the couch?

But Kris realized he would probably survive hearing Arianna moaning and screaming when Xavier had sex with her. But the thought of that man marrying the love of his life was unbearable. When that moment came, he wasn't sure that he could stand in silence anymore.

Kris knew that wealth and good looks wouldn't move Arianna. She valued kindness and hard work. She had respected him, once upon a time, and he liked to think, maybe even been in love with him. And perhaps, if not for Pamela's presence, he might have pursued her properly. But she never deserved to play second to any woman, so he never approached in that way. Man, if he could turn back the hands of time, he would do a lot of things differently. There was a time when he would sing to millions of screaming fans that swooned at the sight of him. His XXO days were the best time of his life and when he was at his prime – confident and on top of the world. That is the man that Arianna deserved to have in her life, and that's the man she was going to get. Yes, he did miss singing and performing. He even missed his band members. But nothing compared to the hole that was left in his heart when presented with the thought of losing Arianna for good. His heart wouldn't survive that kind of heartbreak.

"Since I promised her that I wouldn't get home very late," Kris answered smoothly, checking on his watch. "I have to go."

"Go? Kris, it's ten-thirty. Did Arianna give you a curfew?" Chen demanded in disbelief. "Good God, that woman is a damn control freak. Don't tell me she has your bowel movements scheduled too?"

Now that was funny because he wouldn't put it past her to know that type of sensitive information. "Ha! It wouldn't surprise me if she did." Kris answered with a smile, imagining himself and Arianna in the shower afterward. He shook his head to clear the untimely thought. "Come on. I'll take care of this."

After pulling a few bills from his wallet, the brothers stood up from the table. As they made their way out of the restaurant, all eyes were on them. The brothers made a handsome pair, each very different in their appearance, but striking in their own individual way. Because of Kris's more movie star features, Chen had resigned himself to always coming in second, but without any misgivings, because he got his fair share of the lady's attention. Some women liked the strong and silent type.

"Do you plan to reach out to dad?" Chen asked as they stood in front of the restaurant waiting for valet service.

"Yes. I need to make amends for any hurt I may have caused all of you." Kris said with a heavy sigh. "That's why I asked you to join me tonight. I needed you to know that I am no longer drinking and that I want a relationship with the people who mean the most to me. You're my brother, and I love you."

"I know. And we all love you too. We are ready when you are ready." Chen was sympathetic and changed the subject. "Who's to say no one in there took a photo of you back at the restaurant?" He nodded at paparazzi beginning to approach them. "Speaking of the devil, here come the sharks."

"Damn it," Kris muttered, ushering Chen back inside the restaurant. "I told her to wait until we're done."

"Arianna's only doing what you told her," Chen pointed out. "You need the publicity, right?"

"Yeah, but it doesn't mean I have to like it." Kris turned away from the glare of the flashbulbs.

The valet arrived with Kris's fire-engine red sports car, and the brothers made a run for it, ignoring the shouts and calls from the paparazzi to give them a nice photo. Then somewhere within the small crowd, someone shouted, "Alcoholic!"

As Kris gunned the engine, Chen stuck his head out of the window and yelled back, "Do you kiss your mother with that mouth?" He didn't like people judging his brother.

They burst into laughter as Kris drove away from the restaurant, easily shifting gears. "Damn, I missed you," he said, glancing at Chen with a warm smile before turning back to the road.

"Missed you too, Bro," Chen said. "The Woo duo is back in action." He struck their childhood signature pose, "Swag."

Kris smiled at the memory. "I can't wait to get back into the recording studio again," he admitted. "I've written a lot over the past year. There's got to be a hit or two in the pile."

"I can't wait to see you back onstage," Chen shook his head and agreed. "You've always looked good up there. It's where you belong."

Kris was quiet. His thoughts drifting back to Arianna. "Hopefully that's not the only place I belong."

Chen sighed. "Hell, I'd be happy to find a girl who wants to love and marry me instead of just running off with my wallet."

Kris chuckled. "That's asking a lot."

"I'm serious!" Chen exclaimed. "I think I've reached my saturation point. I'm not saying no to casual sex, but I'd like to come home to someone special. I crave the intimacy of getting to know a woman on a deeper level, you know like making love. Really, it's so tiring going home with a different woman every night."

"I'm not a woman."

"No, you definitely are not. But you're prettier than Arianna." Grinning mischievously, Chen asked, "So, I know she's engaged to that guy. But have you seen her naked?"

She has the sweetest looking nipples and a trimmed little kitty. She's thick in thighs, and I'd be happy to live the rest of my days on my knees for her. "Of course not."

"Why not? With legs like that, she's got to be keeping a sweet little secret in those pants. Tell Arianna the next time I see her, she'd better be in a skirt." Chen smirked. "A mini-skirt."

"Tell her yourself." Kris laughed at the thought. "That would be interesting." His smile was genuine. "She's always thought of you as a dirty little man."

"I love curves on a woman. Hell, if Xavier hadn't snapped her up, I would. Arianna Holiday has keeper written all over her. Those curves are a treasure."

Kris cast him a side-eye. "I don't follow."

"First, she's definitely loyal, just look how devoted she is to you. Second, she's self-made, and I don't think dad would be able to scare her off. And thirdly, that sweet chocolate brown skin of hers is as smooth as silk. The way I see it," Chen finished with a shrug, "she's got good genes."

"'Good genes? What the hell," Kris howled. "Did you just hear yourself?"

Chen ignored Kris and kept prodding. "Then, there's the fact that if we reproduce, we'll populate the planet with our beautiful Blasian babies with rabbity front teeth."

"Hey." Kris frowned at him. "Watch it. That's my friend you're talking about."

Chen held his stomach in laughter. He'd been trying to get Kris riled up, and it worked. "Seriously, you've never thought about having sex with her?"

"Come on. Stop that."

"What? Now that you're a free man and she-who-shall-not-be-named is gone with half your money, you should think about going for it."

"Chen."

"You remember Tyler?"

"Your sour-faced assistant who needs to be put in his place?" Tyler was probably the rudest, most-foul-mouthed person Kris had ever met. But Chen vowed the man knew how to keep Chen's business affairs in order.

Chen clapped his hands. "I'll be sure to pass that along. Anyway, now that you're back, I'd like to repay the hermit's hard work by arranging a meeting with your manager and my assistant."

Kris turned the corner a little too hard, and both brothers were forced to lean to the right in unison. "What the hell? You can't be serious. He's your assistant. And Arianna's..." He turned to glare at Chen. He hated to finish the sentence but spat out the distasteful fact anyway, "She's engaged, you idiot."

Chen shrugged. "I'm sure like any other hot-blooded lady, she's dreaming of a last free ride before diving into matrimony."

"No. No. No. If that's your intention, hell no."

"What if I were to introduce her to..."

"Chen!"

"I'm sure..."

"Don't." Kris warned, "Even. Think. About. It."

Chen turned to his brother, about to make a smart comeback. Then he saw the twitch under his eye and the stiff set of his jaw that was a tell-tale sign for a mounting temper. *Aha! Gotcha.* Chen waited until Kris maneuvered his way around a sharp turn before speaking again.

"Kris, do you like her?"

"What?" He tried to look offended. "Of course not!"

Chen didn't believe him at all. He knew a jealous man when he saw one. "Really?" He said, raising an eyebrow in his direction.

Kris tried not to overreact and look calm. "You're ridiculous."

"No, you are."

Kris just about had enough. "I have no problem with dropping you off in the middle of the road," he threatened.

Unfazed, Chen shrugged. "I have my phone and my good looks." He tried one last attempt to get Kris to admit his attraction. "So, do you volunteer as Arianna's last free lay?"

That was it! Kris hit the brakes.

Silence.

Chen was wisely quiet for the rest of the drive. Kris was grateful. He wasn't scared to face the truth about his feelings for Arianna, but he didn't want anyone picking up on it yet, especially his brother. The merciless teasing was not his main issue. It was the fact that Arianna should be the first to know. He still remembered too well what happened the last time someone else discovered his secret.

He pulled the car in front of Chen's house. As Chen unbuckled his seatbelt, he said, "I'm sorry if I touched a nerve."

"There's no need to apologize, but next time, I suggest we talk about something else," Kris said.

Chen nodded. He should have known better than to push his brother too hard. He was always serious about what he said. But Check could help but chuckle at the fact that Kris had actually stopped the car and ordered him out. Chen had laughed before he realized he was serious. *Yep, he's in love. He would never get that defensive of some random chick. This can't end well.*

Kris left Chen standing at the door of his townhome and headed in the direction of his own temporary home. He had a thirty-minute drive ahead of him and a lot on his mind.

Despite his brother's pushing and prodding, Kris was actually eager to get home, even if it was with Xavier and Arianna. Propriety and common sense told him to make arrangements to move out soon before he overstayed his welcome, but Kris's heart was ready to wait for the shit to hit the fan. Because as long as they remained unmarried, he still had a chance. One argument would do it. He only needed a single window of opportunity. The old him would have created a big ass window a long time ago. But the last year had taught him patience and to have a little faith.

Arianna lived in the suburbs. She hated living in the city and was willing to leave earlier to drive to work. Kris, until last year, couldn't imagine living outside the hustle and bustle of the city. Home was his family's house until college. Sadly, he returned only once. The quiet life of a small town used to make him uneasy, but two weeks in the suburbs had proven Arianna's rationale. It wasn't as quiet as he thought it would be, and the peacefulness helped him piece back together his tattered life, he could think. And it didn't hurt that Arianna also lived in a gated community that protected his privacy and kept paparazzi from camping out.

Kris was cruising down the street where he would have to make the last turn to Arianna's house. When who would he see but the woman herself. There was no mistaking her for anyone else - he would recognize the full, rounded shape of her ass anywhere and those legs. Chen might curse humanity for inventing pants but not Kris. Not leggings, anyway. God, her legs were so long. It was dark outside, her leggings were black, but he was able to make out every curve and jiggle of her thighs. *Good god in heaven.*

She was slowly jogging ahead of him, lost in the motion of her legs and feet hitting the ground. The night was cool, but she wore only a long-sleeved workout shirt, now marked with splotches of sweat on her back. He gently tapped the horn, and she whirled around, her hazel eyes wide, then squinting. He was quick to lower the lights as she shielded herself from the glare. Recognition dawned on her face, and she approached his passenger side window.

Her hips didn't oscillate in that seductive way women seemed to, but her strides ate up the ground, and he couldn't look away. He lowered the window as she bent at the waist.

"You're home?" she said. Her face was flushed and gleamed with sweat. She looked naturally beautiful without a single hint of makeup, and the sight of her beautiful smile made his chest tighten. Her eyes were a golden hazel and seemed to glow in the night light. Her brown hair was piled into a messy bun on top of her head. The neckline of her t-shirt was so high that it was disappointing. But he smelled her sweat, and, dare he say it, moonlight on her caramel skin. The whiff of leftover perfume was cool and aromatic, mixing with her personal scent, had him taking a deep breath to brand his memory.

"You're out late. Can I offer you a ride?"

She smirked and opened the door. "I think I will take you up on that kind offer. I was almost out of spunk anyway."

"I didn't know that you like to run at night," Kris said as he resumed driving. With the window shut, her scent drifted through the car. God, she smelled like moonlight and woman - a warm, sensual, and alluring woman. He was grateful that his pants and the inside of the car were dark, or else Arianna might think that he was a pervert.

She shrugged nonchalantly. "I was feeling restless."

He forced a grin and gritted his teeth. "Xavier isn't distracting enough?"

"He had to leave."

"Oh." *So it is just the two of us tonight.* The though brightened his spirits.

Kris pulled into her driveway and followed her out of the car, admiring how her pink and black shirt hugged her body. Her curvy frame looked soft to the touch. He watched her jog to the entry and punch in the code to unlock the door. Under the sleeves of her t-shirt were dark, round patches of sweat.

He was seeing everything that women usually hide from men. That's how comfortable they were with each other. Lord knows that she had seen him at his very best and at his very worst. So, even sweaty with no makeup on, Arianna was still the most beautiful woman he had ever laid eyes on.

His pants were beginning to grow tighter by the second.

"How's Chen?" Arianna asked as she unlocked the door and went in.

He followed her, forcing himself to stop leering at her rear. "Infuriating as ever but he's family, so I have no choice but to love him," Kris replied as he crashed on the couch. He kicked off his shoes with a sigh then put his feet up on the coffee table.

Arianna took a bottle of water from the kitchen and drank. He had to look away from the motions of her throat swallowing. When she finished, he turned back to see her returning the bottle to the fridge.

"Social media is buzzing about you," she told him, leaving the kitchen so she could sit on the ottoman across from him. She toed off her running shoes. Her socks then put her feet up on the table as well, her legs resting beside his. *God, was that a birthmark on her ankle?*

"You really did call the paparazzi on me?"

"It's my job. I'll show you what the buzz is saying from my iPad a little later."

"Where's your phone?"

She blushed, and that intrigued him. "I dropped it, and it broke. I'll replace it tomorrow."

"Show me tomorrow. Actually, never show me." Kris said, leaning heavily against the couch. "I'd rather read about myself when I've done something worthwhile, not because I've made the first step in bringing back the man bun."

Arianna's laugh was a cross between a chuckle and a snort. Her eyes looked golden and bright as they regarded him. "I take back what I thought about your stupid hair. It works."

He grinned. "Told you."

"And you will do something worthwhile, Kris. I promise." Then her cheeks warmed again. Suddenly, she shot to her feet, picking up her shoes and sneakers.

Surprised by her sudden movement, he asked, "What's wrong?" He could feel it. For the first time since knowing her, a look of uncertainty crossed her features. The amusement in her eyes was replaced with something similar to despair. Kris straightened up, tensing.

"I don't know if this is a good time to mention this or not, but..." Arianna began, revealing a tremor in her voice. She looked at her bare toes as she spoke. "Oh well, I'm sure there will never be a good time to say this."

Kris couldn't imagine what she had to say that make her look at him like that, almost with fear, like she had disappointed him. At the very moment, he was looking at her. Arianna ran her hand down her stomach.

"Oh, god. Are you pregnant?" He groaned, jerking to his feet.

"What? No!" Arianna glared at him.

"You did this." He mimicked her movement.

"That's because I didn't have dinner."

"You didn't have dinner, and you're off running? What if you fainted? What if you fainted and someone kidnapped you? What kind of idiot goes running in the dark starving?" Kris ranted, his dark eyes staring at her with disbelief.

"What the hell is wrong with you, Kris? Will you sit down?" Arianna asked calmly. She looked somewhat perturbed at the combination of his anger and concern. "Because this isn't easy for me."

Trying to avoid what felt like pending doom, Kris tried to put the focus on her again. "You're the one about to faint from starvation. Why don't you sit down?"

"Ha! It would take more than one missed meal to end me. Now, sit down so I can finish."

He glared at her challengingly.

She stared right back and patiently waited for him to comply. When he sat back down, she put her sneakers down and sat on the coffee table. She looked worried as if she was about to relay some really bad news. She leaned forward and looked him directly in the eye. "Kris, I want you to know that what happens next is entirely up to you. I believe in you and your talent," she said passionately, her eyes seeming to plead with him to believe her. "I hope you don't stop because you are one of the greatest artists of this generation. I swear to you that I will work my ass off to bring you back to the top where you belong. Because I honestly believe that is where you belong. You're one of my best friends, and you deserve better. Much better." Suddenly, she burst into tears. "I just don't want you to hate me." Her face crumpled. She just couldn't stop.

Confused but worried for her, he put his hands on her knees and stroked her soft thighs up and down. "Hey. What's going on exactly?"

She let out a loud, broken sob, and he took her chin between thumb and forefinger. Her breath was unsteady puffs from her red nose. He stared at her searchingly, looking into her teary golden eyes, her mouth curved down as she struggled from making any more sobs. His other hand climbed to her cheek.

"Stop that. Tell me, kitten."

A fresh bout of tears fell down her cheeks. "Stop calling me that."

Despite his concern, he smiled. "But it suits you."

"No, Kris."

He laughed and wiped her tears away with his knuckles. "I've never once complained about the names you call me?"

She sniffed. "This is different."

"Nothing you can do will make me hate you, Arianna." He pushed back the sweaty tendrils of her hair from her forehead as he spoke. "How dare you doubt me?" His voice was gentle, even smiling.

Arianna hung her head. "Oh, god."

If he couldn't convince her with words, there was another way.

Kris once again took her by the chin so she would look at him. He looked in her eyes, at the devastation in her face.

Then he kissed her.

Her lips were soft, but he knew that because of their full, plump curve. It took everything Kris had to keep the kiss quick, too quick, reserved, and quick. He stopped himself from licking her just in time, pushing himself away from her with painful reluctance. He sat back, his heart a furious thump in his chest as he struggled from licking his own lips to have a taste of her that remained there.

She stared back at him, cow-eyed.

He schooled his expression into an unreadable mask. "See?" He said blandly. "I clearly don't hate you."

"Not yet."

"Why don't you let me prove you wrong?"

She took a deep breath and squared her shoulders. "Kris, we're friends, right?"

He nodded. "Always." His hand fell on her knee, his eyes on her face. "You'll never lose me."

"I would like to believe that."

"Let me prove it to you."

The saddest hazel eyes in the world stared back at him.

"I broke up with Xavier," she blurted out. Kris narrowed his eyes at her. She hadn't meant to tell Kris about her break up. It had just slipped out. She then took a deep breath before telling him the real news that would bring him crashing to the ground.

"And the record label decided to replace you in XXO while you were in rehab."

Well damn. He hadn't expected that.

Two hours later, Arianna stared at the ceiling in her bedroom. The house was silent, and sleep was avoiding her like the plague. Once again, she punched and pushed at the pillow.

Hours had passed since she killed Kris's dreams, but every time she closed her eyes, she saw the flicker of hope vanishing from his eyes. It was awful, just awful. Arianna cursed the ratched entertainment company and the other band members for putting her in this position. Then she thought about kicking herself because she could have forced them to break the news to Kris themselves. They all had been friends longer, and she felt like it was the company's obligation.

Sighing once again, she made a vow to take on fewer things in the future. Especially things that killed someone else's dreams. How could they do this to Kris? Easy I guess. The music industry was fickle, and fans would turn on a scandalous musician violently. When word got out about Kris's stint in rehab, he quickly became a liability to the company and XXO. So they cut their ties for the greater good. But what about Kris? Well, she wasn't going to throw him away like that. Ever. She planned to stick by his side.

At three in the morning, Arianna gave up on sleep and left the bed. It was a waste of time to search the bathroom for sleeping pills because she'd flushed her prescription down the toilet when Kris moved in. The wine was also kept at a minimum, so the temptation to get drunk was not an option ever. Milk! She remembered. Warm milk. Maybe with a dash of cinnamon and sugar too. That might work.

She tried to move silently as she tinkered in the kitchen. She rinsed the saucepan then put it on the stove. The milk in the fridge was less than half full, just enough to fill a mug. She poured the cool liquid into the pan, found the cinnamon, and sprinkled a few dashes on top.

She was about to bring the mug to her room when a rough groan came from Kris's room. She froze. He was struggling to sleep too. So she turned on her heel and tapped softly on his door.

A startled, husky voice answered her. "Arianna?"

"Yes, it's me. Can I come in?"

The sound of rustling sheets followed. And just when she thought he must have been talking in his sleep, he called for her to come in.

Kris had turned on the bedside lamp and was rubbing his eyes from the glare. As he removed his hands and looked up at her from the futon, his eyes grew wide.

Oops. In her concern for Kris, she realized what she was wearing. The lighting may be limited, but there was no disguising the thinness of her t-shirt and the fact that the only bottoms that she was wearing were panties, though they were the big, full style grannies favored. Despite clearly being sleepy, alertness reached Kris's eyes when he stared at her nipples.

"I have milk." She said, setting it down on the table. "It's yours if you want it."

He sighed and sat up. Arianna looked away from his bare chest and dark nipples. The blanket puddled at his trim waist.

"Can't sleep either?" he asked.

She looked at her feet then him. "I'm so sorry."

"Arianna," Kris said impatiently. "I told you none of this is your fault. I've admitted to God and myself that I had a serious problem. I also learned that part of my recovery includes taking responsibility for my actions and the consequences that occur as a result. My behavior caused harm and embarrassment to my family, my bandmates, the company I worked for, and you. And for that, I'm sorry."

She nodded and turned to go.

"You woke me up, and now you're just leaving?"

She shrugged and presented the mug again. "I have milk," she said, not knowing what else to do.

Kris's eyes burned at the sight of her breast, "Well, if you're offering, bring it over here."

Kris's obvious interest in her chest made her feel self-conscious, especially when her nipple hardened in response to the attention. Arianna took the mug and went to him.

Kris watched her put it on the bedside table, but when she turned to go, his hand caught her by the wrist. "Where are you going?"

"Kris, I'm not really dressed." She was blushing heavily.

He rolled his eyes and released her hand so he could get the milk. "You're a free woman now. There's no point in hiding yourself from me. Please don't leave." He suddenly begged, taking a sip of the milk. Then another. "Damn, that's good. Sit down, Arianna."

She did, but further down near the end of the bed. After all, it was the watching hour, and she was irritatingly aware of her half nakedness.

He needed her to relax. "No. Not at the foot of the bed. Next to me." Seeing her suspicious stare, he held up his hands. "I promise I won't take advantage of you unless you ask me too." He wagged his eyebrows. "No matter how tempting you look."

"Tempting?" She had to laugh. "Yeah, right." To prove that she trusted him, she scooted closer to him. To her surprise, Kris put the blanket around her, handing her the mug.

After accepting the mug, she asked. "Why did you do that?" She asked in confusion.

"It's cold." He nodded pointedly at her nipples. He grinned. "You want me to warm them up for you?"

"Kris." She warned him, hating the butterflies that fluttered in her belly at his offer.

"I'm joking. Try some of that milk. It's good. What's in it?" He lay back down, turning on his side to look up at her.

"Cinnamon and sugar," she added. "I like the smell."

"I know you made it for yourself, and thank you for sharing. Go ahead. Finish it," he urged her, nodding at the mug in her hands.

"I should go back…"

"Stay." At her stunned look, he said it again: "Stay, Arianna. I need my friend."

She knew he didn't desire her, but in light of what had just happened with Xavier, it just felt wrong. She hadn't let Xavier touch her in weeks – since Kris came to stay. He's accused her of pushing him away, but at the time she didn't understand her own lack of interest. Now her brain finally understood what her heart already knew.

And at this moment, her body refused to budge an inch away from Kris. Instead, she lay down next to him on the small bed. It was a tight fit, but after some shifting and turning, they both fit snugly into a perfect spoon. Arianna put the mug on the nightstand and turned off the light.

"Just for tonight," she told him. She was having a difficult time coming to terms with the revelation of her emotions and needed time to make sure everyone was on the same page. He couldn't see her swallow in the dark. But she felt the warmth of his body, the soft hairs of his legs as they tickled her bare ones. She wiggled around, her back against his chest.

"Maybe a few more nights," Kris's voice softly pleaded.

He put his arm around her waist, and Arianna closed her eyes as he kissed the back of her neck. The embrace felt so natural and soothing like home. After a moment, he pulled her closer into him.

Comforted by his gesture, she whispered, "I really do believe in you, Kris. Always. And I will always love you. We are going to blow your solo career out of the water. I'll do whatever it takes to help you make your dreams come true."

Her words helped to stitch the pieces of himself, that had gotten torn and ragged after hearing the news, back together again. He kissed her again on the shoulder this time. "I know, and I appreciate everything you do for me.

But right now, having you in my arms is the one thing that I've always wanted. I knew that we'd be a perfect fit."

"Wait. What?"

"Oh, Arianna. This may not be the most appropriate time to say this, but I need you to know that I love you."

She stiffened in his arms, but he held her tight against him.

"I hid it out of respect for our friendship and your relationship with what's his name, but now that he is out of the picture I can't waste another minute without telling you how I feel." He sighed. "I don't expect you to do anything with what I am telling you. I just needed you to know that I will be in your corner no matter what. I will love and protect you always. You make me a better man."

"Oh, Kris." She intertwined her fingers in his fingers that were holding her desperately. "I've loved you for years, and I think that Xavier knew it before I did. That is the real reason we never got married. He said that he felt like he was only getting part of me. That part of my heart belonged to someone else. Of course, I denied it, but deep down, I knew it was you. I could never let go of you." Somehow it felt easier for both of them to confess this way. Safe in the dark, speaking into the air but anchored to each other.

He groaned and buried his face in the back of her hair, hugging her close out of relief and overwhelming happiness. "Oh, Arianna, you have no idea how long I've wanted to know how you felt but was afraid to ask." He smiled into the darkness. "I swear to never ever let you go again. I need you like I need to breathe again and again. Please let me just hold you tonight. We can discuss anything you want to discuss in the morning, but for now, I just want to hold you in my arms forever."

"There is no place I'd rather be."

THE END

Dirty

DIVORCE

AMBW ROMANTIC COMEDY

AMBW PRESS
ASIAN MEN BLACK WOMEN BOOKS

DIRTY DIVORCE
AMBW ROMANTIC COMEDY

WRITTEN BY

KAY LEE & LOVE JOURNEY

CHAPTER 1

McKenzie Gray graduated at the top of her class from the Indiana University McKinney School of Law and delved into the lucrative world of divorce immediately after passing the bar exam. As the daughter of prestigious African American law professors, she was groomed for the legal field from birth. While searching for career options, she discovered that almost 50% of married couples in the United States divorce. That statistic equaled job security in her eyes, so she set out to become the best divorce attorney in Illinois and was currently at the top in her field. She was a caramel brown, five foot five inches tall, slim in the waist, thick in the thighs powerhouse when it came to moving divorce cases through the legal system. She wasn't sure but felt like something was in the water because this last month had been busier than most.

She listened to the final tick as the clock struck five pm.

She leaned back in her office chair and let out a long, loud sigh of relief. "I'm so glad this week is finally over."

Now, she was free to start her relaxing weekend officially. Her office was a complete mess, with stacks of papers everywhere. Every surface was covered in files, documents, and post-it notes.

Her brain was tired, feeling as overworked as her feet did in those heels. She had been involved in the legal battle of the year, and her office was part of the aftermath. It looked like World War I, and she wanted no part of it anymore.

Suddenly, the intercom beeped for attention. Wrinkling her nose, she grudgingly leaned forward and pressed the button to talk.

Before Lesley, her legal assistant, could speak, McKenzie asked, "Why do people get married?" She shook her head as she looked around at the catastrophe of her office. "Anyone that wants to get married should be court-ordered to look at my office."

Lesley chuckled. "Amen, Sister." Then she clicked her tongue. "I hate to bother you at closing time on a Friday, but there's a man on my other line, one who insists on speaking with you, McKenzie. He wouldn't leave his name, but says it is quite imperative that he speaks to you." The way she phrased it showed the slightest glimpse that she found the man annoying.

Good. She wasn't the only one. Closing her eyes, the lawyer shook her head in disbelief. How did anyone think it made sense to call any business on a Friday evening? Perhaps an emergency dental appointment, sure. But a divorce lawyer? Ridiculous.

Not a single part of her wanted to hear about the stranger, no matter how much they wanted to talk to her. No money was worth her chance to finally relax. McKenzie's voice dropped to a whisper. "No, no, no. Tell him I'm gone and take a message. I'm determined to get out of here at a reasonable time tonight." She shook her head again in dismay. "I will call him back on Monday."

"Will do."

McKenzie released the button and lifted her arms up to stretch. Lesley was excellent with clients, a woman with endless patience, so McKenzie knew she could handle the caller.

Or so she thought. Suddenly the intercom beeped again. McKenzie pressed the button, and Lesley sounded frustrated as she sputtered, "McKenzie, maybe you should take this one. He sounds agitated and just threatened to take your ass to court if he didn't speak with you immediately."

McKenzie took a deep breath. She'd dealt with self-righteous men before. Lesley, please tell Mr. No Name I won't be available until Monday. We can talk about court then."

This time she didn't drag her feet. Grabbing her purse, she climbed up onto her feet and headed out to the front of the office. She'd learned the hard way in the past that saying you're out of the office and not necessarily out of the building could start friction if she was caught.

Lesley was hanging up the phone and shaking her head. "Umm. Hmm. He was livid." She offered a tight smile.

It was the weekend. Couldn't people just relax? McKenzie shrugged, urging her up. "Well, get your stuff, and let's go before he calls back. He's probably one of this week's ex-husbands." She waved her hand towards the door.

Lesley furrowed her brow. "What about the mess in your office? I was going to help you straighten up."

She made a face. "I changed my mind. I hate to start my week disorganized, but it can wait until Monday. After surviving this week, we both deserve to start our weekend as soon as possible. Let's go."

The other woman nodded, hesitantly obeying. McKenzie started turning off the lights and was opening the door for her assistant when the soft ring of the telephone started up again.

Lesley picked up the pace, and they hurried out the door. Giggling, they listened as the ringing stopped. "I'm glad we are leaving together. I'd hate for some angry ex-spouse to jump out of the bushes at you. Who knew the divorce business could be so dangerous?"

McKenzie laughed. "Please stop watching those horror movies. They will have you jumping at your shadow." They stepped into the waiting elevator. "We work in a secure building, and no one is going to shoot the assistant."

"Haha, very funny. What are you doing this weekend?" Lesley inquired, clearly not interested in talking about any more horror stories. Besides, Saturdays were more fun than business conversations or ex-spouses.

Grinning, McKenzie sighed and leaned against the wall. "Absolutely nothing. My couch, TV, and a threesome. Ha, I was just kidding! I'm going to use this time to recover from all the stress this week. What about you?"

"Vihn and I are taking the kids to the amusement park," Lesley said as they exited the building. "Have a good weekend!"

McKenzie waved goodbye as she started walking to her car. Her black pumps clicked loudly against the smooth pavement. At five-five, she always wore heels to court so that her male colleagues couldn't intimidate her with any height advantage. She'd had enough of that during law school. The rhythm clacked through her brain as she made it to her car. Being a lawyer was great, but it required a lot of mental energy. She started the car and paused to reflect on the past week.

Being a divorce attorney was a difficult job. Divorce brought out the worst in people, and as an attorney, she was forced to deal with all the ugliness — the lies, deception, and betrayal. That pledge to love, honor, and cherish went out the door for a lot of people after they exchanged vows.

Someone was always on the losing end, and it was her job to make sure that it wasn't her clients. People divorced for every reason under the sun - infidelity, money, lack of communication, or lack of love. Her last week had been full of back to back divorces that all grew extremely nasty.

As she pulled out, her eyes drifted towards the building again, and she stopped the car. The ground level was made of glass, so it was easy to see the man pacing at the security desk. After what looked like a heated discussion with the security officer, the man threw his fists in the air angrily.

But he wasn't getting past security. McKenzie squinted, trying to recognize the man. He was tall and dark-haired, but that was all she could see. He didn't look familiar. Then her thoughts wandered, and she realized it could have, must have, been the mysterious caller demanding to speak with her.

"Yikes," McKenzie muttered, but she wasn't interested. It was the weekend, and she needed a break. Just a few days without people yelling. So, she turned and quickly made her way home.

People didn't get that furious that fast, though. Something was going on with him. She considered turning back but told herself no. He could yell at her on Monday if he really wanted to. Why would anyone be upset with her? She was just doing her job.

But it didn't matter, McKenzie told herself. That was Monday's problem. Now, it was a Friday night, and she was going to treat herself like a queen. No one was going to ruin her weekend. She'd worked too hard for it. Hopefully, he would calm down by Monday.

AMBW PRESS ASIAN MEN BLACK WOMEN BOOKS – VOLUME 1

CHAPTER 2

The next morning was sunny with beautiful blue skies. McKenzie woke up with a long full stretch in her large bed well-rested. No alarms interrupted her, and no text messages. She grinned, taking her time to get up.

After a hot shower, she decided to sit outside on her back patio. It had been a while since she'd enjoyed some fresh air and sunlight. Pulling on a pair of white shorts and a tank top, she padded across her wood floors to brew coffee. Noticing some dust, McKenzie considered sweeping.

Maybe later. She shrugged off her responsibilities, needing the break. The coffee was made, and she grabbed some toast before settling down with her phone to read through the local news.

It wasn't work, she told herself and clicked the announcements section of her local paper, drawn to the divorce section. She counted them. Two hundred and two were filed the other week. Then she counted the ones she professed herself, which were forty-four. That was more than any other attorney.

McKenzie smirked. She was proud of her accomplishments, despite the hardened heart that she had been forced to develop in her profession. And she was good at it. Someone had to represent these couples during the worst time of their life, so why not make good money doing it?

At thirty-nine, she had a beautiful home and plenty of money in the bank. McKenzie was able to stand on her own two feet and even send money to her mother. With the way people were jumping in and out of marriage, she could count on job security for a long time.

"But enough of that," McKenzie hummed.

Putting the phone away, she picked up her mug and walked out to her backyard. Summer was finally fading. Her yard was neatly trimmed by a landscaping company, along with the trees that provided her privacy to enjoy quiet moments like these. The September morning offered clear skies, and the warm air smelled like peonies.

She moved across the patio and sat in her chaise in the sun. Working indoors so often meant that she was in desperate need of Vitamin D and a vacation. Reclining, she lifted her coffee mug to her lips and took a sip. She grinned. A smooth French vanilla blend just the way she liked it. Life couldn't get much better.

Settling the coffee mug down, McKenzie settled in comfortably. The sun felt wonderfully warm and had a way of smoothing the aches in her muscles and the wrinkles in her forehead. Her eyes closed. This past week had worn her out. In a matter of moments, she was asleep.

Then the sound of her doorbell ringing jerked her awake. Jolting up, McKenzie winced and rubbed out the kinks in her neck as she turned towards the house. Even from her spot in the back, she could hear it ring again.

It would have been possible to ignore her unannounced guest if they didn't insist on ringing the damn bell over and over again.

Gritting her teeth, she stood up and wondered who would be so annoying this early on a Saturday morning. "I'm coming," she called, "Keep your pants on." McKenzie glanced at the coffee mug, and instead of traipsing through the house again, she took the shorter path past her fence to her front porch.

A tall, dark-haired man was pacing there. For a moment, he looked familiar, but then he didn't. When he glanced in her direction, she noticed his beautiful Asian eyes and hesitated. She'd never seen him before.

That didn't matter as he went back to her doorbell and rang it again.

She could feel a migraine coming on. Forcing a polite smile to her lips, McKenzie called out. "May I help you?"

The man turned, inhaling deeply. Moving over to the railing, he leaned forward and looked her up and down.

"Are you McKenzie Gray?" He demanded. Red blossomed across his cheeks and wasn't the most flattering look for him. She tried not to think about the rest of his features as she focused on his face.

"Yes, I am." Her eyes narrowed, wondering how a stranger could look so disgusted with her. It was a Saturday morning, and the world was minding its own business. Why couldn't he?

Stomping down the steps, he came closer. "Gray, the attorney?"

She dropped her arms. This was about business? No one from work came to her house. How did he know to go there? McKenzie nodded slowly, hoping that she'd gain an understanding soon. "That's right. What can I do for you?"

His dark eyes flashed, sending a tingle down her spine. She tried to ignore it, especially as he raised his voice, throwing a hand in the air. "Do you have any idea what you've done? Any idea!"

A twinge of fear trickled down her spine, and that's when it hit McKenzie. She hadn't heard his voice, but she'd seen the man at the security desk. It pieced together perfectly. This was the man who'd desperately wanted to speak to her. Swallowing, she took a step back. Perhaps she should have stayed. But how was she supposed to know the man was crazy enough to show up at her house?

Throwing her hair back, McKenzie pulled herself together. To avoid feeding his emotions, she kept a controlled tone. "No, it looks like I don't. But I'm willing to talk. Please lower your voice so we can talk about this like adults."

"Now?" He spat. "Now you want to talk? What, yesterday wasn't good enough for you?"

She took a step forward. "You can talk like an adult, or you can leave. Why don't you tell me before I call the police to remove you from my property?"

He spun around in a circle and ran his hands through his hair. "Go ahead!" He offered. "Of course you would say that. You're heartless and cruel, so I wouldn't be surprised that you of all people would do something like that! Call everyone, why don't you? The police! The army!"

At that moment, they heard her neighbor's garage door open. Out stepped Latrice, who immediately glanced over and waved. "Hey, McKenzie!" The tall blonde paused, looking surprised. "Khoi? Is that you?"

He froze. The man dropped his arms. His frustrated scowl softened as he waved. McKenzie watched, dumbfounded, as her beaming neighbor hurried over. "Hey, Latrice. It's good to see you. How are you? How's Darren?"

McKenzie watched as the man's mannerisms changed. Speechless, she couldn't even move as she watched the conversation unfold.

Latrice waved a hand. "Oh, he's good. He's out golfing, as usual. But I didn't know you were here! When did you get back?"

"It's funny, you should ask. I actually caught a flight back into town yesterday." He winced, shooting a glance at McKenzie. "I've been back for one day, and it's fascinating all the drama I came back to. Of course, that's all thanks to Kaara and your neighbor here."

McKenzie straightened. Latrice had called the man Khoi, but she couldn't remember anyone she'd talked to lately named Khoi, or even Cory or Coy. No one at her work was named that, nor any of the files she'd dealt with that week.

But there was a Kaara, wasn't there? She blinked, thinking back just as her stomach began to sink. It was a slow and slimy road down as a bitter taste settled in her mouth. What had that case been about? She tried to remember.

Latrice gasped as she put a hand to her heart. "Oh, dear. That wasn't you and Kaara in the divorce column, was it, Khoi?"

Khoi was quiet for a minute before grudgingly saying, "I'm afraid so."

McKenzie held back a gasp as she finally remembered. Kaara Cai. The case she had questioned so many times because the circumstances were so out of the ordinary: a Quit Claim Deed to all property, a substantial settlement that was mysteriously uncontested.

Kaara had been the one client she'd recently dealt with who she'd been reluctant to handle and had struggled internally with for the entire case. It had been complicated to prepare, but almost too easy in court. There wasn't a word from the husband, Teion Khoi Cai Kaara had called him Teion. Something had seemed suspicious. But there was so much to work that McKenzie had trusted her client, done the work she could, and moved on.

She put a hand over her mouth as she stared at Khoi. Teion. Teion Khoi Cai, or whatever he called himself. The man continued chatting casually with her neighbor as though nothing was wrong, as though he hadn't been screaming at her a minute ago.

"When did this robot move in next to you and Darren?" He asked suddenly, giving a disgusted nod toward McKenzie. She glared back.

"Oh," Latrice laughed good-naturedly as though she thought it was a joke. "You're too funny. Lawyer jokes are just ridiculous. But she's a darling. McKenzie here has been our neighbor for almost a year now."

He sighed. "That's unfortunate. But at least I'll have good company while I'm in town. Tell Darren I'll see him later. Maybe we can get out on the greens again, just like old times."

"Oh?" Latrice clapped. She was a sweetheart, even if she still acted like a peppy cheerleader. "That's wonderful!" Latrice replied enthusiastically. "That's just great. Well, I'm afraid I have to get going. Are you staying at your house?" She started back towards her house.

Khoi waved. "No, actually. Not yet. I've decided to stay here until I get my house back. See you later, Latrice!"

"Hope that doesn't take long. Bye!"

"I agree. Bye!"

As he waved, McKenzie felt a knot form in her stomach. Crossing her arms again, she wondered what his comment meant precisely. The man turned to her with a bitter smile. "It better not take long. In the meantime, you won't mind a house guest for a few days, will you?"

CHAPTER 3

Somehow McKenzie was speechless again. It took her a minute to gather her thoughts.

Shaking her head, she told him, "I don't know what you're thinking, Mr. Cai, but I can tell you here, and now you're not stepping foot inside my home! In fact, I.. I will have you forcibly removed if you don't leave this instant."

He scoffed and walked right past her, brushing against her shoulder. She fell back a step and whirled around as he walked through her open gate. McKenzie squawked a protest and hurried after to find him pulling open the back door.

Every step looked so normal, from the way he walked. If she didn't know any better, she would think the man lived there.

But he didn't. She rushed around the corner after him, panicked. "What are you doing? I said to leave! Get out, or I will call the police!"

Once inside, the audacious man started to touch everything. He went around the living room, testing for dust on the television and glancing at her plate of toast crumbs. "Go ahead," Khoi cut her a hard stare. It was so harsh that she jerked to a stop, her eyes wide.

"Fine, I will," she responded, trying to pull herself together. But she was barefoot and confused as this stranger wandered around. "I'm going to!"

Khoi snapped, "Good. You might as well call the press as well. They'd love this story. A married man comes back home and is greeted with no wife, no house, and no money. Just wait till I tell them that it was all your doing.

"They'll love to hear about everything you did while I was out of the country, thousands of miles away, working to aid world peace. Then when I return to my house and what do I find? No house. No nothing. I can't wait till everyone knows the illegal underhanded tricks you've pulled. Go ahead and call the whole town! Maybe we can get Oprah. It's going to be a big story, you know! A big one!"

McKenzie shook her head, growing more frustrated by the second. He opened cabinets in the kitchen, and she trailed behind to close them.

Finally, she slammed the final cabinet shut and roused to battle pitch. "What I did, Mr. Cai, was follow the letter of the law. I have done nothing illegal or immoral. I merely presented my case before the court, and they moved on the evidence presented. If you have a complaint, then move in with the judge!"

"No, thank you," he circled the living room. "Judge Spivey isn't really my type. Not only is he a fraud, but he's a fat fraud with no shame. But you?"

McKenzie stopped when he stopped. The man eyed her, making her face redden. "You're cute. Maybe just what I need to soothe the terrible injustice I've suffered. Besides, your house smells amazing. Yes, you'll do nicely."

She was busy trying to unload everything he'd just claimed as he opened her front door and unloaded his luggage in her hall. Two large suitcases and a computer bag. Her mouth dropped as she finally realized he was serious.

His piercing eyes narrowed on her. "Don't worry, you'll get over it. Everyone makes mistakes. I'm just giving you the chance to fix it. I'm not going anywhere. Not to jail, not to my house, not anywhere until you sort this out. I want my house and my car back. I did have a car, you know. But Kaara has that now through that fraudulent performance you two put on. Did you hear the word fraud, by the way? That's the keyword, lovely. Fraud."

Houses could be cleaned, and items could be replaced. But the moment he claimed her work was indecent, McKenzie was done. "Look, Mr. Cai, I haven't done anything to you! Not a damned thing!" She marched over to her phone and waved it. "But I am going to... right now! You have one minute to remove yourself and your possessions!"

Taking a deep breath, McKenzie glanced down at her phone and repeated, "One minute."

He shut the front door. "Are you threatening me?"

"Excuse me?" She didn't mean to shout, but she did. "Am I standing in your house? Am I trespassing on your property?"

"Okay," he nodded slowly, "you aren't threatening me. I forgive you."

The man was done yelling, but she wouldn't have it. She couldn't believe him. Somehow she choked out a bitter laugh. "You forgive me! What a joke. No wonder your wife divorced you. You're crazy!"

But she stopped short as he marched over until they were inches apart. "Sure, that's it. The strain was too much." He spoke softly. "My nervous system collapsed. I can't sleep or eat or do anything. My loving wife left me and claimed full ownership over my home, my car, and all my money. When I landed and learned I couldn't use my credit card, I called the beautiful woman. And you know what she told me?"

McKenzie backed away from him cautiously, her hand still grasping the phone. For the most part, so far, he'd kept his distance. There had been the shoulder shove in the yard, but that was it. Now, he was so close. Her stomach tightened, and she wondered if she could remember anything from her self-defense classes. He didn't appear the violent type, but McKenzie was nervous.

He continued as though it wasn't strange to move into a stranger's home. "She said that if I had a problem, I'd have to go through her attorney. Guess what? That's you. So darling attorney, here I am. Go ahead. Call anyone you like. I don't care. As to the charge of being crazy, I assure you, my most insane moment was at my wedding when I said, 'I do' instead of 'no way in hell.'"

Her lips twitched, but it was her lawyer's stance that kept her from chuckling. This entire situation was beyond ridiculous and almost funny. But then McKenzie remembered she was angry, and she glanced at the phone in her hand.

Thinking fast, McKenzie looked for a solution. Calling the police didn't appear to be helpful. Perhaps she could lend him something to make it right? She started talking as she thought through it. "Look, I apologize for any inconvenience you may be experiencing, but it does give you the right to barge into my house." She closed her eyes and took a visibly deep breath. "Alright, I won't call the law yet, but you can't stay here," she said. "I'll call you a taxi, and you can go to a hotel."

"I don't have any money," he reminded her and crossed his arms.

"Then I'll compensate you for the weekend," she forced herself to say. "But I don't think it's appropriate for you to..."

He scoffed, taking a step back. "There's nothing appropriate about any of this."

Typically, under pressure, she performed very well. But as he gave her his intense stare, McKenzie could hardly remember her own name. "Uh... listen, do you have family here?"

"Does an ex-wife count? Though the more appropriate word would be thief or criminal. She committed a crime, remember? With your help."

McKenzie threw up both hands. "You had a chance for your case!"

The man scowled at her. "Tell you what," he said after a moment of them staring at each other. "I'll compromise. Monday, I'll look for an apartment."

She took a step back as he hefted his bag onto his shoulders. It looked heavy. "Why not today?!"

"I'm tired," he replied softly. He slumped now, his anger fading. McKenzie stared uneasily, noticing the dark circles under his eyes. "I've flown thousands of miles to get here. I haven't slept in days or eaten anything."

McKenzie grasped at straws, trying to think. "Look. The only reason I am even talking to you is because of my integrity as an attorney. I value justice and feel for your... inconvenience. But I didn't agree to this."

"I didn't agree to anything either," he pointed out. "Now, do you have a spare bedroom or not? You owe me this much, Ms. Accomplice to Perjury."

She was tired and confused and upset. This was supposed to be her weekend. She hadn't had a weekend without work in months. And this is the type of shit that shows up on her doorstep?

But under the circumstances, she didn't know what else to do. She stomped her foot. "Fine! But if you even think about. about touching me or my things again, you're gone! And on Monday, you are out of here! Understand?"

"Where's the spare bedroom?"

She crossed her arms over her chest. "First door on the left."

CHAPTER 4

The man dragged his bags down the hall. They rolled noisily over her polished wood, grating on her nerves. As he opened the door, she heard him say, "I've always wanted a pink room. It's so cozy."

She clutched the sides of her head with her hands. How could this be happening! In America! In Illinois! To her! Her wildest imagination wasn't enough to envision this predicament. Staring at the empty hall, she shook her head.

McKenzie was pacing when she felt herself being watched. She paused and found Khoi, a tired expression on his face. "Do you mind if I fix myself some breakfast? I haven't had much of an appetite since I landed yesterday." As he spoke, his eyes moved down to her top and lingered on her breasts.

An involuntary blush came over her face, and she yanked fiercely at her top, pulling it up. It wasn't like she'd expected company. She gave him a threatening glare. "You may sleep in my spare bed, use my kitchen, but don't get any ideas that I'm included in your petty scheme. Keep your eyes off my body," she ordered firmly.

He winked at her. "Don't worry, darling. I have serious doubts that I could find a lawyer who stole all my worldly possessions appealing. You're as safe as if you had a large wart on your face." Chuckling to himself, he walked toward the kitchen.

Deep inside, she knew she had made a serious mistake letting him stay, but she refused to admit that to him or herself. What else could she do? There were laws against this, but that wasn't her specialty. And there was the smallest ounce of guilt eating at her. McKenzie was struggling with her own hesitation to put an end to this crazy situation.

Her shoulders slumped as she listened to the man's movements with the opening and closing of cabinets, the clanging of pots and pans. A moment later, she heard butter sizzling in a pan.

It triggered her into action. Wait! This man was blaming her for all his misfortunes. Misfortunes that he brought upon himself. How could she be held accountable for that? Bolting into the kitchen, McKenzie placed her hands on her hips. "You do realize, don't you, Mr. Cai," she said firmly, "that a lawyer must rely on a client's truthfulness and honesty? We don't have the time or resources to investigate each client beyond the basic case."

Holding the iron skillet handle, he glanced back. "McKenzie, dear," he said mockingly, "I thought we weren't going to discuss the case. Now be a sweetheart and let me eat my eggs without choking on more lies." A slow grin covered his lips. "Or did you come because you wanted to sample my cooking?"

Her face flushed. "No!"

"It's a cheese omelet. Are you sure?" The grin widened.

"No!" she snapped again. Looking at the empty egg carton, she exclaimed, "Did you use all those eggs?!"

He shrugged. "It wasn't a full dozen."

Her mouth parted, then she raged, "Almost! It was at least nine!"

The man loosened the top buttons on his white shirt. "Are you begrudging me a few eggs? Me, the golden goose who laid Kaara's golden egg?"

They stared at each other.

She studied his clipped, coal-black hair and the long straight nose beneath it. He had a wide mouth with mockingly full lips and a firm jaw with a strong chin. He was lean, cocky, and aggravatingly attractive. Her heart fluttered in chest uneasily, and she had to look away.

Spinning around, McKenzie closed her mouth and left the kitchen.

"Where are you going?" he called.

She didn't reply.

In the hallway, McKenzie rubbed her forehead as she felt her inner calm deserting her. No other ideas came to mind. She didn't know what to do with him. Though she understood she could evict the man, and file a restraining order against him, for some reason, she didn't feel it would help. It might even stoke the fires of disaster.

It had been a long time since she'd felt so useless. What was preventing her from doing anything? She should have called the police thirty minutes ago. That's what any sane, reasonable person would have done. It was still an option. So, why wasn't she doing it? Was she afraid that he would ruin her reputation?

This entire situation would definitely bring unwanted and unwelcome scrutiny. And it could make her a laughingstock among her colleagues. Damn, it! She had worked too hard and long to end up as the punch line of any kind of freshman mistake type joke. Besides, her neighbors knew him and knew that he was here, so there was a bit of security.

Sighing heavily, she went into her bedroom for a moment and locked the door. The man was humming now, and her migraine was in full force. It was time for some quiet. And maybe this would turn out okay. McKenzie wasn't sure how, but she was out of other ideas. Perhaps she could tolerate this arrangement until Monday.

Lying on her bed, she tried to think. But her eyes kept flitting to the door, checking that it was locked. She was listening for his footsteps. Straining to hear what he was up to. Maybe he was robbing her. She tried to think about what critical personal items she had left outside her bedroom. Nothing came to mind.

For the rest of the day, McKenzie hid in her room. It was not the relaxing day she had hoped for. She didn't clean, she didn't bake, and she only fell asleep around sunset for an hour when her head ached so much that she couldn't see straight.

The migraines had been a problem all her life. Ever since she was eleven, they came when she was too stressed or overworked. It was one of the reasons she'd been so ready for this weekend. Miraculously, she'd spent the last month keeping them at bay. There was no telling how long they'd last. Sometimes an hour, sometimes a week.

When she ran out of water in the glass she kept by her nightstand, McKenzie knew it was time to venture outside the safety of her bedroom. Lord knows what that man had done to her house while she was holed up in her sanctuary. The house was hers, after all.

CHAPTER 5

McKenzie's hands shook as she forced herself out into the hall. She squinted in the hallway light he'd left on and flipped the switch off. The pounding in her head grew as she slowly carried her glass to the kitchen to refill it.

"You're not dying, are you? That would be inconvenient."

She jumped, nearly dropping the glass. McKenzie groaned, forcing herself to look at him on the couch. He had his feet propped up, his own glass resting on a coaster and his computer on his lap. The man really did act like he owned the place.

Her head hurt too much to bother with him now. Telling herself, he had to be halfway decent since he hadn't physically assaulted her or called her any names besides Attorney or Robot, McKenzie sighed. "Just be quiet, all right?"

Then she turned to the sink and winced as she turned it on. Even that was too noisy. Biting her tongue, McKenzie glanced around her kitchen as she realized some food might help. As though it was listening, her stomach growled.

"I made quesadillas if you want one," he informed her. "They're on the counter."

"I don't want your food," she started and stopped. "My food. Never mind. Just... just keep it down, will you? And stop leaving the lights on. There's no need to be such a rude houseguest."

As McKenzie moved achingly to her pantry, she heard the slap of a computer shutting and his footsteps trailing to the kitchen. Soon she could feel him watching her.

He cleared his throat. "Herniated disk?"

McKenzie glanced back at him with a frown as he insinuated she was hobbling around. "Of course not. I'm the picture of health."

"I didn't know lawyers had human illnesses," his eyebrows raised as he offered her his mocking smile. "It was that or a migraine. I've seen the symptoms before.

Did you take any Advil? Or are you an Ibuprofen kind of woman?"

Waving a hand in the air, she pulled out a loaf of molasses bread. "It's an ergotamine, I believe. I don't remember the name."

As she moved to get the butter, he tutted. "Well, if that's not working, you should probably try a triptan. Or did those not work for you?"

Slowly she spread the soft butter across a slice of bread, raising one shoulder in a shrug. If she didn't lift or move her head in any direction, then it wasn't so bad. For a minute, McKenzie considered not answering. It wasn't his business anyways. But it was his fault.

"My doctor said to give this a try first, then we'd consider other options," she mumbled. "What are you, a doctor?"

"Yup."

McKenzie jerked in surprise, dropping the knife, almost hitting her foot. But luckily, it missed and landed loudly on the ground. She winced at the loud noise before squinting at the man leaning forward with his face in his hands on the counter.

The man chuckled to himself as he came over and picked up the knife, putting it in the sink. He'd since rolled up the sleeves to his shirt, and her eyes slid up his fine, thick forearms. Her throat tightened, and she forced herself to look away.

She watched as he washed his hands, then he explained himself. "I joined the Marines to pay my way through medical school. I worked in a DC hospital as an ER doctor afterward before realizing I could do more good. So, I bought the hospital and used the proceeds to fund the building and maintenance of hospitals in Africa."

He glanced back at her with a bitter smile. "I had just finished up the third in Sudan when I came home to find my dear, darling Kaara had decided to take everything and run. With your help, of course."

"I'm not apologizing," she told him. "And I promise to burn your computer if you talk any louder."

"Can I quote you on that?"

McKenzie picked up her buttered bread, one of the only things that didn't make noise when she ate it and made a show of grabbing one of her chopping knives, showing it to him, and then walked out of the room.

She was just getting back into bed when there was a knock on the door. Groaning, McKenzie shook her head. "No, Khoi."

He knocked again. "You left your water out here."

Swearing under her breath, she grudgingly climbed out of bed. Picking up the knife, she unlocked the door and opened it a crack. Khoi offered her the glass and waved an object around in his other hand. "Also, I soaked a cool rag for your forehead. Had some lavender oil on hand as well that helps with relaxation."

She made a face, staring at the rag. At first, she wondered if it might be chloroform, but she could already smell the flowery scent. "Are you one of those all-natural doctors? The ones without real medical degrees?"

For some reason, he chuckled. It was like his anger from that morning had dissipated. "You don't get to be in the Marines and believe that. But herbs have some healing benefits, and it was a gift from one of the women in my clinics. Here."

"You're being nice to me," she pointed out as she grudgingly took it. Now her hands were overly full. Glass in one and a knife with a warm rag in another. "Be careful, it might become a habit."

Chuckling, the man shook his head. "Don't worry about me. Just get some rest. You look dead on your feet."

Yes, because of you. Instead of responding, she shut the door in his face. McKenzie stumbled back into bed after setting everything down on her nightstand. The sun was setting, and the natural light was fading. She gulped down the water and ate half the bread before deciding it was all she could manage for the moment.

Closing her eyes, she decided to try the cool rag on her forehead. It was cold, but it smelled pleasantly sweet. McKenzie sighed, the tension in her shoulders fading away. The pounding in her head eventually softened, and she found herself falling asleep.

CHAPTER 6

The following morning, McKenzie woke and wondered if it had all been a dream. She stared at her ceiling, waiting with bated breath. Surely her imagination had run wild. There was no way she would have let a stranger barge into her house, let alone stay.

As she took personal inventory, she realized that the migraine was gone. McKenzie changed into a new pair of shorts and tank top before she glanced back at her bed and found the rag lying on her bed. She hesitated before picking it up. It smelled of lavender. *Damn.*

Grudgingly, she grabbed it along with her bread plate and cautiously left her room. It had been a long time since she'd lived with roommates. Even now, she remembered how complicated it was to live with other people and wrinkled her nose. Her first big splurge after graduation had been to rent her very own apartment.

The occasional guest, like her mother, was acceptable. A man she hardly knew, however, was not.

Her eyes skirted the couch and kitchen, but he was nowhere to be found. His computer wasn't there, and his messes were cleaned up. The more she glanced around, McKenzie realized that the house wasn't dirty at all. She sniffed, wondering if she smelled lemon. *Had Khoi cleaned?*

Everything was silent as McKenzie washed her plate, put the rag in the laundry room, and looked for something to do. The house remained quiet as she showered, changed, and returned to the living room to sit on the couch.

Though she attempted to clear her mind of all her work, Khoi's complaints from the other day continued to bother her. So, she gave in. It felt likely the migraine would return soon, and she wanted to get some research done before it overtook her.

Grabbing her laptop, McKenzie headed out to her back patio. Tying her thick brown hair in a knot on top of her head, she started looking into Kaara's file.

"Do you always dress so modest?"

She pulled her sunglasses down as Khoi walked up, slurping a smoothie. Then she frowned as he set a second one down on the table beside her. Like he'd made an extra one for her... with her own food.

Then her eyes drifted down to the short shorts and her light top. "It's my house, remember?" McKenzie offered her usual glare. "My yard, my clothes, my body."

Deciding the conversation wasn't exciting enough, he changed the topic. "You were up early today."

"And you were up late," she countered. "Did you finally come to your senses? Realize that you've been a selfish jerk?"

"At least I'm not a slob." Khoi took a few steps out onto the grass. He was dressed more casually in jeans and a short-sleeved button shirt and looked like he'd used her hallway shower. His hair and tanned skin glistened in the sunlight.

She pushed her sunglasses back up. "So, what are you up to? Working? If I'd known you were just waiting till Sunday to work, I might have..."

His voice grated on her nerves. McKenzie interrupted. "I'm going over Kaara's case files, thank you very much. Since you're throwing such a fit, I thought I'd look into it." Then she gave him a good stare. "And if you don't shut up soon, I'm calling the police."

"Go ahead," he shrugged. "But enjoy the smoothie first." And then he strolled back inside.

Irritated, she shook her head and tried to concentrate again. Everything was clean and legal. Everything was as it should be. She'd gone through the files three times now to make sure she hadn't missed anything.

But she could hear Khoi in her head now, and it was distracting. All she could see was his clever smirk and his bright shiny grin. Then she remembered their conversation from the night before. He was a doctor. A doctor who worked in Africa.

Why wasn't that in the papers?

McKenzie frowned at her computer. That should have come up. His money, his employment, all of his assets. Clicking around, she dove in and found nothing. The assets were in America, everything the wife had wanted. Kaara had bypasses on the other information, stating it wasn't anything out of the country, so it wasn't irrelevant.

Maybe there was fraud. Her heart skipped a beat. It couldn't be. Her record was so clean. She grabbed her computer, paused for the smoothie, and headed in. "Khoi! Come here."

He trailed down the hall. "You rang?"

She forced herself to swallow an angry retort. Tucking a pen in her knot of hair, McKenzie waved a hand. "Get over here. You were pissed yesterday, and if you want to get this sorted out, then you're going to tell me everything."

"Oh? Now you want to listen. Did you hit your head? It's those migraines, I'm assuming, or whatever illegal drugs you probably got from someone."

At least he wasn't screaming. Rubbing her temples with both hands, McKenzie shook her head. He was pissed at her for ruining his personal life, and now he didn't even want her help. The man was clinically insane. She wondered if she could call the hospital to come to take him away. They might have restraints or something.

When she opened her eyes again, Khoi was sitting down in the chair across from her. He glanced down and fixed a wrinkle in his shirt. It was a nice shirt, and she realized the pattern was filled with stethoscopes. She'd thought they were giraffes. Her lips quirked up until he looked up, his dark brown eyes staring her down.

McKenzie turned back to her computer. "My work is immaculate. You should know that from the beginning. I take my work seriously, and I trust my clients. However, that doesn't guarantee honesty. And that's not something I can spend a lot of time looking into with all the cases that clear my desk. You take what you can, learn what's there, and make a call. When it comes to divorce, there tends to be a loser and a winner. That's just how it is."

"Because you make sure of that," he shot back.

She raised a finger. "I asked you to be quiet, so stop taking shots at me and stop talking until I say I'm ready for you." Brushing a few fallen curls from her face, McKenzie sighed. "As I was saying. I do my work with integrity. But the justice system isn't perfect, and things can go wrong. I've seen it before, that's just the way it is. While I can't share with you all the files, I can talk you through some information I have, and we can look into your options."

The man straightened up and crossed his arms. Her eyes wandered over the toned muscles and wondered if he worked out. Then she blinked. "Fine," Khoi agreed. "What do you have?"

It was a tense situation that left McKenzie with a tight stomach and a dull headache. But she wanted him gone, and part of her wanted to make sure that she made an effort to do the right thing. While there was nothing she could have done in this situation since her client had lied to her, part of McKenzie still felt guilty that this had happened.

Not that she felt terrible for Khoi. He deserved this for the attitude he had. But she didn't like her clients tricking her, and she hated the idea of having helped a deceitful person. McKenzie rubbed her hands together and started asking him questions about his work. The types of paychecks he received, how he paid taxes, what sort of international income he might receive, and so on.

As they talked, she found herself asking him more personal questions like how he'd wound up where he was. Khoi told her about the children he met, the families he helped, and the good he wanted to do for the less fortunate. He ordered Chinese takeout for two from his favorite place in town, which she paid for, but at least the food was delicious.

Soon they were both sitting on the couch together, having finished their food, and still talking. It was nearly midnight before they glanced at the clock again. She was rubbing her forehead again, feeling a familiar ache, when he let out a low whistle after checking his watch.

"It's almost Monday," he wrinkled his nose.

"Good," she offered a sleepy grin. "Then, I can kick you out in a few minutes."

He glanced up. "Oh, did I say I'd leave this Monday? I meant the next." They stared at each other before grinning and then looked away.

Somehow in the midst of their conversation, she didn't know exactly when but called a truce. The anger was gone.

Khoi cleared his throat and stood. "Besides," he changed the topic, "You should get to bed. It looks like that migraine of yours is threatening to return. Did the lavender help?"

Putting the computer away, McKenzie yawned. "Hm? Oh, I don't know. I fell asleep shortly afterward, so I don't know. You know what, it's fine. I just... I need to go to bed. I should be back in the office early, after all, and..."

By the time she trailed off, he'd prepared another cold rag and put it in her hand. "Take it." There was a slight military time to his command.

Not sure if she liked it or disliked it, she asked. "Are you ordering me to take this rag?" Her eyes narrowed.

He considered it. "As the doctor in the house, yes. Now go to bed." And he walked back to the kitchen before she could think of a response. She bit her tongue. Just as she thought things were almost okay between them, he did something rude and obnoxious.

But the ache was quickly becoming a migraine, so she gave in this once. Taking the rag, she picked up her water glass and went to her room. Maybe ignoring him would make him realize how rude he was.

"Tomorrow," she sighed as she climbed into bed. "I can worry about this all tomorrow."

AMBW PRESS ASIAN MEN BLACK WOMEN BOOKS – VOLUME 1

CHAPTER 7

"You what?!" Lesley screeched when she heard the news.

McKenzie laid her forehead on her desk. Technically it was a pile of papers since there was no available space on the desk she hadn't cleaned up before the weekend. But it didn't matter. She just needed a moment.

On the other side of the desk, her assistant paced around the room. McKenzie could practically hear the woman's panic. It matched her own nervous heartbeat. How had this all gotten so complicated?

"But... but... but... how?" Lesley tried to ask. Anything else she said was mostly gibberish. Clasping her hands on top of another pile of papers on the desk, the short woman stared at her with wide eyes. "How did this happen? Why didn't you call the police?"

Though McKenzie opened her mouth, nothing came out. "I didn't know what to do. He... he's a rather convincing man."

Lesley gave her a skeptical look. "You're a lawyer! The top lawyer in Springfield, Illinois, McKenzie. You could have surely, I don't know, argued him out of the house? Have you done something? But he stayed the night! Two nights! Is he at least gone now?"

Jerking her head up, McKenzie realized she didn't know the answer. She looked at Lesley through wide eyes, trying not to freak out. He hadn't made a sound all morning, and after being in a hurry, there was no time to see if he was still around.

"I don't know," she admitted. "I have no idea!" Groaning, she rubbed her eyes. "What's happening to me?"

"How do you not know if there's a stranger in your house?" Lesley's tone grew shrill, but she noticed and lowered her voice. "All right. Here's what we're going to do. We're going to call the police station and have someone check on your house, okay? Then we'll file a report, and you'll take the day off to see a doctor. Clearly, you're having some kind of breakdown and..."

McKenzie groaned, rubbing her temples. She'd been able to ignore the beginning of a headache this morning, but it had ignored her in turn and was growing into a migraine now. "Shhh. Just... just... give me a minute, please?"

Passing a water cup over, Lesley sat in the seat on the other side of the desk. "You can't just let him stay at your house. You wait long enough, and he might try and claim squatter's rights. That monster has to go. He's bullying you. Drink some water and come to your senses."

"I just... can you give me a minute?" McKenzie asked. Her voice was hoarse, and she couldn't remember if she'd eaten anything that morning. She hardly remembered driving to the office. Closing her eyes, she sipped the water. "And turn the lights off on your way out, please."

Once Lesley was gone, McKenzie opened her eyes in the dimly lit room. She was dressed in the usual skirt, suit jacket, and heels. The blouse she wore was the dark purple one with sequin trim, her favorite. It really brought out the light brown of her eyes. Yet she didn't remember getting dressed. Had she talked to Khoi that morning? Everything was a blur.

Sighing, she glanced at her computer. She'd had these blackout moments before. It was nothing new. But it was irritating. Rubbing her temples, she started to sort through her emails. Fortunately, there was only one internal meeting that afternoon, followed by one with a new client, and that was it. She had the morning to herself.

Though McKenzie tried to ease herself back into her work slowly, her thoughts continuously wandered. Khoi had forced his way into her house and into her mind. Though she hadn't talked him through the details of the case he'd somehow missed out on, the details had consumed her.

Kaara had been a petite Asian woman with long blonde hair. The woman had a high pitched voice and liked to play the victim, carrying around a handkerchief to dab at the tears McKenzie had silently questioned. She'd arrived with all the necessary paperwork filled out, including an addendum stating that she'd made all the legally required attempts to serve the divorce. The documents that she presented seemed in order and showed that the legal deadline to respond to her public announcement had passed - meaning they didn't need to wait for the other party to be present physically.

It was unfortunate, McKenzie remembered thinking, but it was very well put together. She'd done a little online work to glance through the history of the case, even looked for any online presence for Teion Khoi Cai but found nothing. The man was nowhere to be found, and that was enough for them to ask a judge to grant Kaara's request for 100% of the marital assets.

Now that she was away from Khoi, however, she managed to question his claims as well. What proof did he have for his defense? He should have seen those documents months ago. Had he just ignored them? Had he run out on Kaara for Sudan or wherever he was?

"Nothing makes sense," McKenzie mumbled and went over to her cabinet. Maybe she'd missed something in her research that would be in the paper files. "Ha. Here we are..."

Her back wall was all glass, letting in more than enough natural light. She took off her shoes and slowly began to pace around the room in an attempt to remember everything she could from the case. Even pulling out the voice recorder she used for notes, McKenzie replayed everything.

Something was off, but she just couldn't place it. Rubbing her forehead, McKenzie tried to think of something to do. Then it struck her. She'd been skirting the issue the entire time, walking around in circles. All she had to do was talk to Kaara.

Grabbing her desk phone, McKenzie found Kaara's number and called. Rubbing her forehead, she glanced at the empty water bottle and was about to use her intercom for Lesley when the other line picked up.

"Kaara here," a familiar voice rang out.

"Kaara, hello," McKenzie forced herself to smile. "Good morning. It's McKenzie Gray, your attorney. How are you doing this fine Monday?"

The woman chuckled. "I'm doing just great now that we finished out my case. I can't believe it worked out so well. My life is definitely improved! Cheers. So I spent the whole weekend celebrating, a trip to the city and everything. But enough about me, darling, what can I do for you? Did I leave something at your office again?"

Straightening her posture, McKenzie tightened her grip on the phone. "No, actually, this is about your case. I know it's been settled, but I wanted to double-check some information with you. For example, do you remember your addendum addressing how your documentation was never accepted by the other party?"

Kaara's loud breath rattled the audio before she finally said, "Yes. Yes, the other party refused to sign."

"I just need to reconfirm some details," McKenzie assured her quickly. "How many times did you share it? Was it always in person or through the mail?"

"Mail, of course. The other party was out of the country. What's going on here?" The woman interrupted before McKenzie could say anything more. She talked fast like she was beginning to panic. "I wrote everything on those papers you made me write, and we already talked about this. What's done is done, isn't it?"

McKenzie hesitated, trying to remain calm. "Of course, yes, but if any of the paperwork was faulty, you see, faulty with the incorrect information for any reason, purposeful or not, then the entire case becomes void and..."

"What?" Kaara shrieked. "It can't be void! Everything is mine! I told you, everything is right! Why won't you listen to me? What is going on over there? Are you trying to ruin me?"

Startled by the yelling, McKenzie pulled the phone away from her ear. She'd been yelled at before, and Kaara definitely seemed to panic the moment something went wrong, but surely the woman didn't need to act so extreme. "I just need to reconfirm some information, Kaara, that's all. I've talked to Khoi, and he's countering that..."

Apparently, that was a trigger. The woman suddenly screamed. "TEION?!"

It felt like a knife to McKenzie's brain, and she paused, leaning over the desk. For a minute, she stared at her, shaking hands. Maybe she should have waited to call the woman until she'd had some water. Or a snack. It had to be close to lunchtime.

Glancing at her clock on the wall, McKenzie listened to the woman's unintelligible screaming and realized it was already past lunch. She'd spent the entire morning reviewing the case again. In fact, her department meeting was in an hour. No time for food now.

"Now Kaara," McKenzie tried to wedge in.

But it didn't work. "I can't believe you! Why are you talking to him? You can't trust him! That... that jerk! You're supposed to be on my side! Mine! That's why I paid you! I want my money back," and she started into a stream of expletives.

At this point, the money wasn't worth it. McKenzie started to pace again but grew weary and leaned against the desk again for support. She wanted to hang up on the woman, but she still needed details. Just a few answers. A few words to confirm that everything was right and legal.

She tried again. "Kaara, I need you to listen to me, okay? I'm on the side of the law. I'm doing my job. I just need to double-check, okay? Even if something is incorrect, we can fix it. We can take it back to the judge. I just need you to be honest with me."

Kaara didn't appear interested in that, however. She screamed one more time and abruptly hung up.

Stunned, McKenzie put the phone down and rubbed her temples. This had done nothing to help her migraines. She groaned and was about to step out and grab a bottle of water when she noticed someone in her doorway.

"Looks like you could use this," Khoi offered, tossing a water bottle at her.

She barely managed to catch it. Sighing, she wiped her forehead and fanned herself as she gulped down half of it. "Thanks. And what are you doing here? How did you get here?" Still recovering from Kaara's sudden harpy-like attitude, McKenzie tried to pull herself together. Didn't she need to tell him something? She tried to think clearly, but she wasn't feeling well.

The man sauntered in, glancing around her office. McKenzie frowned as he settled into her office chair. Not the chair of a guest. Her chair. The one she had specially ordered upon receiving this office. "By way of Sergeant McNeil. Apparently, someone called the police that I was at your place and tried to kick me out."

McKenzie blinked. "What? Oh, Lesley..." she set the water bottle down and went to peak out her office door to find her legal aid still at the desk. She couldn't blame Lesley. The woman was just trying to help.

"I didn't ask her to do that," McKenzie offered after a heartbeat as she tugged at her heavy jacket. "But you did say you would leave. Wait, then how are you not in jail?"

She didn't really want the answer, but she needed a distraction from the migraine.

He offered her that familiar smirk. "Sergeant Andy McNeil and I go way back. We're old friends from college. He offered to give me a ride wherever I wanted, and it gave us some time to catch up."

Sighing, McKenzie shook her head. Then she winced as her skull began throbbing. Still fanning herself, she looked towards her vents and wondered if the air conditioning had stopped working. Surely Lesley would have mentioned something, wouldn't she?

"Anyways, he dropped me off here and said he could give me a ride later after his shift. I think we'll catch dinner tomorrow."

McKenzie stopped listening as she remembered the water on the desk that Khoi had brought her. Maybe that would help, she told herself and hurried over to pick it up. But she moved too quickly and grew light-headed. Picking up the water bottle, she noticed her hands were shaking. Again?

That was the last thought she had before everything went dark.

CHAPTER 8

McKenzie didn't know exactly what it was that woke her up. Maybe it was the steady stream of beeping. Perhaps it was her sore throat. Or possibly the feel of rough cotton against her legs.

Whatever it was, her eyes slowly opened as she found herself in a hospital room.

"Where am I?" She croaked, her voice dry and raspy as she tried to sit up. Confused, she glanced around just as Lesley and Khoi reached her on each side.

"It's okay," Lesley assured her and lightly pushed her shoulders down. "Don't get up. You're in the hospital."

And Khoi said, "You passed out an hour ago in your office and banged your head on your desk. There's no swelling in your brain, but you're extremely dehydrated. How's your head?"

She blinked, trying to take it all in. "My head?" Raising a hand to her skull, she felt the tug of an IV. Then she remembered being in the office. The migraines had been getting worse.

Then she winced. The pain was back. Giving up the fight to sit up, McKenzie squeezed her eyes shut. "The lights," she forced out. "Please turn them off."

"Oh, of course," Lesley murmured and scurried across the room.

Then there was Khoi, who tapped on her shoulder. She peeked an eye open, trying not to cry out in pain, and found him holding a cup with a straw. "You've got liquids coming in, but you should try more. It'll help," he instructed. "Here."

She didn't want to be treated like a baby, but when McKenzie glanced at her hands, they were still shaky. Grudgingly, she accepted the straw he brought to her mouth and obediently drained the cup. By then, the lights were off, and she settled back into bed, sighing in relief.

As Khoi checked her screens, she remembered he was a doctor. Then she realized she didn't want him there when she was naked and wrapped in a dumb hospital gown. McKenzie turned over to Lesley, who eyed him warily. "You can go," Lesley told him. "You didn't even need to come."

"I'm a doctor," he pointed out her. "And you were freaking out. I wasn't about to leave the lawyer alone."

"Well, we're fine now," Lesley snapped back. "She's going to be fine. You're just part of the problem. I'm asking you nicely to leave. Don't make me call security. Besides, you were supposed to be arrested."

Khoi shrugged. "I'm too charming to be arrested."

That made McKenzie snort. "Is that what you call it? Why no woman can stand you?"

He scowled at her. "Maybe you hit your head too hard, and the other doctor missed signs of a concussion. I'm plenty charming. All of you are just..."

"Go ahead," Lesley snapped. "What were you going to say?"

McKenzie winced as her migraine grew more aggressive. This time she raised her hand more slowly and tried to rub it away. "As fun as this is, you two, please shut up. Or at least have the decency to whisper." Sighing, she checked her hair. "Where's my doctor? Did he say I could go?"

Both of them shook their heads. "They want to keep you overnight," he started.

"Which she might not need," the other woman stated. "Just because you're a doctor doesn't mean you're right about everything. You didn't need to insist on that."

The man continued talking as though he didn't hear her. "You're staying for overnight observation in case any other symptoms arise, but more importantly, to ensure that you walk out of here healthy," Khoi explained tactfully. "Your CT scan looks good, but it could change, and we want to make sure you're properly hydrated and steady on your feet before you leave."

She groaned and glanced at Lesley, who shot a quick look at the time on her phone. "I canceled your meetings for today and rescheduled them for Wednesday, just in case. The partners said you need to take it easy, so I'm recommending you take a sick day tomorrow. But we could add Wednesday as well. You let know, and I'll make it happen."

Right, work. McKenzie couldn't forget that. She waved a hand at the woman. "I'll be fine on Wednesday. I'm sorry to do this to you, Lesley. Thanks for your help, but since I'm clearly going to be fine, you don't need to stay. I know you don't like hospitals. You can go, it's fine."

"Are you sure?" Lesley hesitated and looked over at Khoi suspiciously. "Maybe I should call security on my way out."

McKenzie bit back a smile. "It's fine. He needs me, so he can't hurt me. I'll call you in the morning?"

It took a little more convincing, but finally, her assistant left. Only then did McKenzie sigh, relaxing into the blankets before she remembered she still wasn't alone. She turned slowly and found Khoi fiddling with a rubber glove in the chair beside her.

"You can go, too," she pointed out.

He shrugged. "And go where? Your house? It's boring when it's empty."

"Then go wander the hospital," McKenzie told him. "You don't need to stay here. You're making me wonder if I was wrong, and you're going to smother me if I fall asleep."

Standing up, the man shook his head. "Fine. I'll take a walk and stretch my legs. But then I'm coming back to keep an eye on you. I'm not smothering you because you're right." He cocked his head and stared at her. "I think I need you."

The man's eyes were breathtaking. They were dark and deep and soft all at once. Her mouth turned dry as she heard her heart monitor speed up. A blush spread across her face as Khoi's lip lifted in the corner.

Deciding to have mercy on her, Khoi saluted her with the glove still in hand. "Get some sleep, would you?" His voice softened. "I'm a doctor, so you know I'm right. You need to really rest." And then he was gone.

McKenzie settled down and closed her eyes. There was no one there now, just her and the beeping machines. Swallowing down the uncertainty and unsettling feeling of not being in her own bed, the aching in her skull grew so loud that it was easy to give in to the sleep that enveloped her.

For the rest of the day, she dozed. In and out of sleep, McKenzie hardly recognized anything except for the scent of lavender. But she didn't think about anything until the sun was setting, and a nurse stopped in to check her vitals.

"You're looking good," the woman assured her. "And I brought dinner." She gestured to the table on wheels. "Since you were so dehydrated, however, we are keeping an eye on your bladder. So, when you need to use the restroom, please use the measuring pan in the toilet. Have you gone since you've been here?"

McKenzie's cheeks heated up at the idea of being assisted in the bathroom. "I'm fine, I told you. And no, I haven't ventured out of bed yet."

The nurse grinned. "That's not good news. It could mean that you are more dehydrated than we thought. Try eating and press the call button when you're ready to go. We'll keep you as long as we have to otherwise," she added as a warning before walking out.

McKenzie's face was still flushed when Khoi strolled in. He was juggling four small water bottles. She paused, her eyes trailing after the moving objects. The man could hardly get any stranger. Dressed casually in a hoodie and sneakers, Khoi reminded her of a Silicon Valley I.T. expert.

But there he was, juggling, and smirking.

One by one, he tossed the water bottles by her feet. She jumped at the first one, but not at the two that followed. Khoi caught the last one. "Ta da!" He posed before dipping into a bow. "Thank you. I'll be here until you start clapping."

"I'm eating," McKenzie protested, wincing at his loud voice. "That's not fair."

There was a Jell-O cup and spoon in her hands. He lowered his voice, remembering her sensitivity to sound. "You're eating hospital food? That stuff is garbage. As someone who spent five years living on it, trust me, I know. We're getting you something else to eat. Where's your credit card?"

"You can't have my credit card," she ordered. But then she hesitated. "Could you hand me my phone? I need to call Lesley. It's in my purse over there. I want her to get me a few things from my house."

Cracking open a water bottle, Khoi grudgingly obeyed. Instead of grabbing her phone, however, he brought the entire bag over. "I was raised not to look through a woman's purse."

"Oh? I've never known such a polite pack of wolves," she mused as she carefully set the Jell-O down. McKenzie tried to sit up and grab the bag, but it was down by the water bottles, and she was hooked up to too many machines, and her blankets were too tight to let her stretch that far. "Khoi..."

He sighed before moving it closer. Taking the seat near her, he slouched over the arms and watched as she sorted through her things.

McKenzie tried to ignore him. After all, her head was still suffering through the migraine that wouldn't leave her alone. It pounded against her skull like an anvil, trying to crash through. She moved slowly, wishing for the thousandth time she didn't have such a big purse with so many things in it.

But finally, she found the phone. She squinted when it turned on, too bright. She turned down the volume and lighting before calling Lesley. But it was nearly six in the evening, and most likely, her assistant was driving home, listening to her favorite romance podcast.

She decided to leave a message just in case. "Hey, Lesley. I was just hoping you could stop by my place and bring me a few things? Not much. I know you still have a house key, and I'd appreciate my toothbrush, some real clothes, and the like. Maybe my computer." She ignored Khoi's glare. "Anyways, just give me a callback. Thanks."

The room fell silent for several minutes as she waited for Lesley to call her back. But time passed right on by.

After about fifteen minutes slowly ticked by, Khoi tried again. "So, real food?" he clambered up, more graceful than she thought appropriate, and rubbed his hands together. "You're not touching that casserole. There's a sushi place down the street I can run by. What do you think? Maybe some rainbow, or spicy tuna?"

Shaking her head, McKenzie settled back in bed. "No, I'm fine. You should get something. But that Jell-O was enough."

His eyes slid over to the empty cup and then back to her. She watched as he studied the bed and then checked her IV. He flicked the bag curiously. "Hey," McKenzie ordered more loudly than she meant. Sucking in a deep breath, she put a hand to her head and gave him a look. "You don't work here, remember?"

"Have you gotten out of bed since you've been here?" Khoi demanded before glancing over at the clock. She shook her head. "You've been here for over six hours. Based on the amount of fluids they've given you, you should have experienced some bladder movements by now."

Her face flushed. "That's inappropriate, Khoi."

Grabbing the water bottles at her feet, he handed them to her. As she grabbed at them, he moved around to the other side and pushed a button, forcing her to sit up. McKenzie groaned. "Would you stop?"

"No," he shook his head. "Not until your body starts functioning. You could lose a kidney or a liver like this. Trust me, I've seen it. There are villages without clean water all over the planet, McKenzie. But you're here with the best care in the world. Now you're drinking all of these water bottles, and then I will get you on your feet if you don't use the restroom in the next two hours."

The next two hours were the most annoying two hours of McKenzie's entire life. Though she attempted to feign falling asleep three times, Khoi never gave her more than twenty minutes of peace. He even brought her nurse back to discuss her fluid intake. To her dismay, the nurse agreed with Khoi's ideas and brought more water as well.

When it struck nine pm, McKenzie protested as he pulled back the blankets. They were tightly folded, but he was a strong man. "But I'm tired," she groaned. "And I'm only in a hospital gown."

Khoi rolled his eyes. "I'm a doctor. Get over it. Now on your feet so I know your body is at least trying to do something. Maybe we'll go get you more Jell-O."

She made a face. "No, that's all right. Bread, though. I'll take bread."

"Bread?" He repeated.

"Bread is delicious in every form, Khoi, got it? Delicious." Then she sighed and grudgingly accepted his outstretched hand. "I can't believe I'm doing this. You broke into my house, and now I'm naked in a hospital room with you."

He smirked. "Funny how life works sometimes. Now, around the room, we go."

"Wait," McKenzie put a hand over her stomach as she stood. Her legs shook beneath her, and her head swam, but it was nice to be on her feet. Then her stomach rumbled. It took her a moment to reorient herself, but then she nodded. "Okay, it worked. You win. I need to use the restroom. Let the nurse know, would you?"

Khoi cheered quietly, giving her a helping hand to the restroom door before hurrying off. McKenzie handled her business and made it back to the bed to collapse. That took all of her energy, just moving across the room. But, she realized, the migraine was lessening, and she was feeling better.

"So, sushi?"

She picked up her phone and shook her head. "No, I told you... Ugh, Lesley." McKenzie called the woman again, but it went to voicemail. She swore under her breath.

"What did you need?" He asked after a heartbeat. "I'll get it for you."

"How?" McKenzie threw him a look.

He shrugged with that smirk. "Your car."

They debated for several minutes. But somehow, Khoi continued to win. Soon she had prepared him a list of items she wanted and handed over the car keys. McKenzie wondered if she was losing her scruples. But Khoi walked out, and she couldn't tell any longer.

An hour later, he returned. Carrying a small overnight bag, he waved it in the air, and then he waved another plastic bag. She grabbed a hairbrush and allowed him to display the food he'd brought. There was some sushi, but also molasses bread, butter, jam, and two croissant sandwiches.

"Variety," he explained.

She raised an eyebrow. "My money."

Khoi settled in his seat after parceling out the food. "Get me my money back, and I'll repay you every penny. With interest, if you like."

McKenzie smirked in return. She would hold him to that. The two of them settled down for the evening and ate. Somehow Khoi had talked the nurse into letting him stay past visiting hours, and he held McKenzie's attention for hours with his stories from overseas, talking until she fell asleep.

In the morning, he returned shortly after she woke up. The nurse checked her vitals a few times, and after a discussion between the three of them, her nurse decided she was free to go. She just needed to take it easy for a couple of days. No action, just a whole lot of calm and rest.

"Why would we go back to the office?" Khoi protested as they climbed into her car. "The nurse said you needed rest. That office does not seem restful, McKenzie."

She shrugged, turning them toward the freeway. "I told Lesley I'll work from home for the rest of the week. I just need my computer, okay? And stop complaining. It's not like you have anything better to do."

CHAPTER 9

The moment McKenzie walked into the office, Lesley hopped to her feet with wide eyes. "McKenzie! Miss Gray! What are you doing? You're not supposed to be here."

Waving her hand, McKenzie sighed. Though the flats and wrap dress Khoi had grabbed from her closet were decent enough for the office, she still felt self-conscious as she crossed the sitting room. "Morning, Lesley. I'm just stopping by for my computer."

Lesley rolled her eyes. "I could have brought that to you. Just because I couldn't help you last night since my phone died doesn't mean I can never help you again. Take a seat, would you? I'll grab it for you. No other case files, right?"

She shook her head, pushing her hair out of her face.

The moment she got home, McKenzie planned to sink down into her tub for a long hot bath. Watching Lesley hurry down the hall, she took a seat on the nearby sofa and sighed. Her office was the closest to the front lobby, which meant she could always hear the commotion out here. Some clients just thought it was the place to rant and rave. Sometimes it was irritating. Why were people so loud?

As though on cue, the doors opened.

Turning, McKenzie smiled and prepared to welcome the next guest into the office. But as she came to her feet, she wavered. It was Kaara Cai. Her stomach dropped. Inhaling deeply, McKenzie noticed the clenched fists, blonde hair, and slightly smeared lipstick.

For such a small woman, Kaara definitely had a way of stomping around.

"You!" She pointed at McKenzie, and a rush of insults flew from her lips.

McKenzie tried to respond, but the woman just needed to calm down, or all hell was going to break loose. Nausea rose in her throat as the headache returned. But she forced herself to remain standing. McKenzie waited for Kaara to stop shouting expletives so she could take a turn. Finally, McKenzie raised her hands, trying to calm the woman down. "Kaara, I apologize for any misunderstanding. I wasn't trying to upset you. Why don't you calm down, and we can go sit in my office and talk?

"Talk?" Kaara shook her head. "We are beyond talking! I'm going to find another lawyer and sue you! You can't talk to Teion. He's a liar. A liar! You're such a stupid..."

Khoi arrived through the front doors, making both women jump. "Kaara Marie Khoi! Are you a harpy or the devil? Stop yelling!"

The woman screamed as though she'd seen a ghost. "What are you doing here? I told you to stay away from me! You jerk! I hate you! You... you're supposed to be in Europe!"

"Africa," he corrected her. "It's Africa. How do you still not know the difference?"

McKenzie took a step back as he raised his voice.

He immediately became the angry man she'd met in her yard. "I can't believe I married you! I can't believe you did this to me! Your case is fraudulent! You're a liar, and I'm sending you to jail if it's the last thing I do!"

Kaara shrieked. "You can't do that to me! You left! Everything is mine. You never wanted any of it, anyway! You didn't care about me or... the house, the car, or any of it! You! Were! Gone! It's over!"

McKenzie took a step back from the shouting match, growing dizzy. But the movement caught Kaara's eye who stood between them. Another scream from her brought a wave of pain crashing through McKenzie's head. She grabbed the couch for support.

"And you!" Her client cried out. "I can't believe you! I hired you, not him! Why are you talking to him! Whatever happened to confidentiality! Why couldn't you just do what you were supposed to do?"

Her vision blurred as she raised a hand. "Kaara, please. Let's just sit down and take a deep breath. We can just..."

"And sit down like we're friends?" The woman laughed, throwing her head back. "No way! I'm getting a new lawyer, and I'm suing all of you for harassment! You'll never work again! Both of you are going to jail, not me! Especially you!" She snapped at McKenzie.

McKenzie wanted to say something in response. To defend herself, her job, her work, something. But she didn't feel right. When she opened her mouth to talk, she tasted acid reaching up through her throat. Hurriedly she turned towards the bathroom but only made it to her assistant's desk to grab the trash can.

She hadn't eaten a lot for breakfast. Just two slices of bread and half an orange. But all of it came back up and landed amongst shredded paper and a banana peel. Nausea clung to McKenzie's stomach as she hugged the can, struggling to remain standing. She was dizzy and hot and tired and felt so gross.

Standing against the desk in a daze, McKenzie lost track of the screaming. But it was loud. A constant noise that grated in her ears. Whatever they'd given her at the hospital had not been enough. Then she remembered she was supposed to pick up a new prescription. That's where she had meant to go after this, before home.

McKenzie wavered, her legs weak. Two hands reached around her waist to steady her. When she looked up, she caught sight of Kaara, leaving in an angry huff. Then she glanced to her side and found Khoi.

"You need to lie down," he scowled at her.

She gestured limply to the couch where she'd been only moments ago. Or was it hours? McKenzie could hardly see straight. Coughing lightly, she allowed Khoi to lead her from the counter where she still hugged the basket.

Lesley arrived with wide eyes and McKenzie's computer case. "That didn't sound good," she muttered. "But don't worry, I told everyone it's not your fault."

"Thanks," McKenzie mumbled, picking hair off her sticky lip. Khoi handed her a water bottle, which she used to wash out her mouth and spit into the trash can. Sighing, she shook her head. "You married quite a woman," she whispered to Khoi.

He took the seat beside her, waving Lesley away. The woman glared at him, but the phones began to ring, so she had to leave. "Kaara used to be sweet," Khoi informed her. "And she has her moments. We married just before I started my clinics abroad, but I'd told her in advance about my plans abroad. All she saw were the big paychecks, though. Then I made my first trip away. I was only gone for three weeks, and she had her first affair. I tried to make it work and understand her loneliness, but things only got worse. I guess that I was too optimistic."

McKenzie snorted at Khoi before drinking some water. She started to tilt it down, but he pushed it back up to her mouth, urging her to drink more. Groaning, she obeyed and drained the bottle before he moved his hand.

After waiting for her to catch her breath, he said, "I apologize for that."

That's when she noticed he smelled delicious. When had he taken a shower? Was it cologne? She couldn't place the scent. But it was lovely.

Khoi put a hand on her shoulder, and she blinked at him. "Between my wife and I, I'm afraid we've terrorized you. But if you could help me, I'd appreciate it. I don't need the car or the house, or any of my stuff. I just need access to my accounts. In fact, one particular account would be enough. Just so I can keep working with the hospitals. They need that money."

Of course, he would choose to be nice now. McKenzie stared him down for a minute before sighing. She knew she would relent but wanted to give him a moment to think about it. There was enough in the last month that she already regretted, so why not add something else to the list?

McKenzie nodded. "I'll help you under one condition. Please take me home."

"Deal." His lips quirked up into that familiar sexy smirk. It was the first time he'd flashed it that day, she noted. But then she flushed and glanced away before he set the basket down, tossed her empty water bottle in it, and helped her to her feet.

CHAPTER 10

"Get back on the couch. That's all I asked you to do. How is that hard?" Khoi threw his hands in the air as she glared at him from the hallway. "You act like I'm trying to put you in front of a firing squad."

She pointed towards the door. "I just wanted to go for a run, okay? I feel good this morning. Can't you just let me enjoy this?" Then McKenzie shook her head. She didn't need to be asking for permission. "Just bring me my running shoes, would you?"

But Khoi shook his head as he sauntered over. He didn't stop until they were nose to nose. McKenzie's creased brow softened as she swallowed, wondering what he was doing. he hadn't yelled at her since that first day. He was a puzzle she couldn't piece together. He could cook, he was a doctor, and he'd beaten her in every chess round but one. What was he still doing there?

"No." The word escaped his mouth softly. He smelled of basil from their morning omelets he'd prepared. Khoi cocked his head, studying her as she stared at him.

She waited, holding her breath, wondering what he was thinking. She swallowed as he raised a hand and buried it in her hair. It was a lot of hair. Not bothering to straighten it while staying at home for the week, McKenzie had let the natural curls flow over her shoulders. Her heartbeat against her ribs and she found herself breathing heavily.

Suddenly pulled something out of her hair. "Saving that for later?" He asked lightly. "We have plenty of cheese."

The moment ended. McKenzie exhaled loudly and felt the tight muscles in her chest loosen as she shook her head at the strange man. "It's my cheese, remember? Now, where... where are my shoes?" She cleared her throat when her voice cracked.

"You're not going for a run," Khoi stated firmly. Then he paused and glanced at the sunlight. "But it is a nice day. A walk would be good for you. Maybe around the block. Just because you feel like you can do it, doesn't mean you can... nor that you should," he butted in when she opened her mouth to protest. "Do you have any idea how many people reinjure themselves because they're feeling fine for a day? Too many, that's what. Put on your sandals and grab your sunglasses. Let's move it."

Unable to help herself, she slumped off to her room to obey. "It's not like you're my doctor," she reminded him. "You're just an obnoxious parasite who won't leave me alone."

"If I wasn't here, you'd be in a lot more trouble," Khoi shrugged. "Besides, I'm charming and handsome. And I cook for you. Your life is probably better than it's ever been. So, I'd show a little more appreciation towards me if I were you."

Rolling her eyes, she grabbed her keys and followed him to the front door. "I thought doctors were supposed to be humble people."

"No, we actually all have pretty big god complexes. However, mine is excusable because I'm actually a good person," he winked as they made it down to the sidewalk. "You're just lucky I decided to stay. If you'd been a hideous beast, I never would have set foot in your house."

She snorted. "Oh, yeah?. Especially since you saw me in a hospital gown. Lucky guy, seeing me at my best."

Khoi waved to Darren, who was standing by his window. "Please, even your worst is better than my ex." They took a few steps before he said anything more. Carrying the water bottle he'd handed her, McKenzie wasn't sure what she should say. "Man, she's a nightmare. I don't even know what I was thinking when we got together."

"Probably, that she was good in bed like most men think," McKenzie mumbled.

The man snorted. "Well, yeah, but... she changed. Trust me, she was a doll once. I met her at a fundraiser for an animal shelter, for crying out loud. But money changes people. When the dollars started rolling in, I bought us a nice big house and put her in an expensive car. Then I realized I had to give back. And she decided she wanted more and more."

McKenzie listened quietly, realizing that he wasn't happy about how his relationship had ended, and he just needed to vent. He'd fought hard for his marriage and done what he could. Left without a choice or a dime to his name, he'd come to her. Though she hated to say it, the man had become helpful.

The previous day, when they'd returned from the office, he'd put her things down and supported her on the way to the bathroom to brush her teeth. Then she was sent to bed with blankets, a fresh lavender towel, and plenty of bread, pills, and water. Since then, he'd taken the role of cooking and cleaning and keeping her company when she woke up.

He wasn't a bad guy. And the more they sorted through the court documents, the more she realized she'd been messed over pretty badly by Kaara... just as severely as Khoi had been. If the other woman hadn't tried so hard to hide everything, then this could have been McKenzie's fault, and she could have lost her license or been barred. But luckily, there was plenty of evidence that worked in Khoi's favor.

"Let's get back to the house," McKenzie decided as they finished their short stroll. She offered him the remaining water in the bottle and realized she was glad he had stopped her from taking a run. He was right. She would have made it a block or two and then probably collapsed. But the morning walk was an excellent opportunity to brief about the case as well. "I need another pill, and then we can go through your flight receipts. We need those and proof of service."

"Okay. And then what?"

It was finally her turn to smirk as they climbed up to her front door. "Then, we go to the judge."

It turns out that there were certain protections for military personnel serving overseas and humanitarian workers in the justice system that prevented these very types of situations. All Khoi needed was proof of his time abroad that showed his inability to be reached in the remote areas where he was working, especially during the times Kaara had shown her fake attempts to make contact.

And in McKenzie's defense, since the woman had already offered three legitimate examples that fell under the legal guidelines, McKenzie had not been legally required to follow up with attempts to contact. But she should have. So now, she was trying to make things right. The two of them sat on opposite ends of the couch, putting their feet in the middle, and grabbed their computers to get to work. Only taking breaks for ice cream and a delightful quiche Khoi prepared for lunch. The afternoon passed by in peaceful quietness.

Well, mostly quiet.

"Your printer is more annoying than anything I've ever known."

She glanced up at the machine on her crowded home office desk. "What? It's fine. She's just... old."

He rolled his eyes. "You named it, didn't you? You're one of those people."

McKenzie kicked his shin. "So what if I did? Besides, you don't have a printer, so no complaining, mister. Or you can leave."

He scoffed lightly, his voice still low. "What? Are you still trying to kick me out? It's not Monday."

Stifling a giggle, McKenzie shook her head before putting one of her file folders down. "I can kick you out whenever I want."

"At this point, I'm never leaving," he warned her. "Besides, you need me here. I don't know how you survived without me. I'm great company, and my Asian persuasion is damn sexy. What more could you need?"

"I don't know," she rolled her eyes. "Someone with a little bit of humility, maybe?"

But he shook his head. "Those people are boring."

"But at least they don't go around reminding everyone how good they look," she countered, waving her pencil around. "You act like you're still in college."

Leaning forward, he winked at her. "Can you really look me in the eye and tell me I'm not handsome?"

"I..." She had half a mind to lie. "Maybe," she dropped her gaze and turned back to her computer before her face could blush. But it was too late. She swallowed. "That's irrelevant, okay?"

"It's okay," he shrugged as he settled back on his end of the seat. "I think you are beautiful, too."

Her lips quirked. "Damn right, and don't you forget it."

He put up both hands. "Gorgeous, fine. Wow, when did my arrogance start rubbing on you?"

"I was like this before you invited yourself into my house."

"All right, that's fair. You know what? I can work with that."

She chuckled and kicked him again. "Shut up and get back to work. We're waiting on one more document."

But that one paper turned out to be trickier than they thought. All he needed was proof that there wasn't any way he could have received an email in the middle of Sudan. McKenzie and Khoi quieted their bickering and started to work harder.

It took them more than thirty hours. She had other work that had to get done before the weekend ended, and he had to reach out to his people in Africa to search for any ideas on how to provide specific proof that a judge would accept.

Friday afternoon, they finally found it. Scrambling, both McKenzie and Khoi dressed and crossed town to find an available judge at the courthouse.

Judge Spivey was running open court again. Khoi hissed in her ear that they could wait until Monday for another judge, but McKenzie wasn't having it. If a judge tried blatantly to allow fraud in the legal system, then he'd be accountable as well. She believed in righting a wrong. And today was the day.

Thank goodness for a slow week. The pair were granted the opportunity to make a quick argument to get filed in between the other cases being presented that afternoon.

They stared at their papers, and McKenzie could feel her hands shaking. The stress was building up again. She sensed a migraine on the edge, just waiting to fall down on her head.

Not now, she told herself. I'm so close. Not now. McKenzie put it out of mind and stood when Khoi's case was called.

Judge Spivey frowned at them. "You're addressing a closed case? You're wasting my time, Gray."

She took a deep breath. "I'm afraid not. My previous client falsified legal documents and made fraudulent claims that void all final decisions. All I need is your signature. I can make my case quickly so we can head home early, or I can spend all night talking about it, your honor." She handed over everything she'd put together with Khoi. "Here's the evidence."

After a few minutes of flipping through the pages, the judge spoke up. "That's a lot," he scowled. But he continued to rifle through the packet. The more he looked, the deeper he frowned. "Well, this is a nightmare.

Is this true?" She nodded. "You've reviewed this enough to know it is all true?"

Again, McKenzie nodded. "I have all the necessary signatures, your honor, as you can see in the final two pages." she glared at him sternly, "And we both believe in justice. That's why I am standing before you today - to right a serious wrong." Her eyes skirted the stenographer before straightening up. "Your honor. This is a matter of justice being served for every person who is serving our country overseas and trying to make the world a better place. If this woman is allowed to strip this upstanding gentleman of everything he owns, then clearly there is little hope for the future. It is our responsibility to ..."

Judge Spivey interrupted her by clearing his throat and a deep sigh as if he was dealing with a headache of his own. "I've seen enough. Let the record show that I've reviewed the documentation that will be copied and shared into evidence for any reference. Because of your newly discovered evidence, the original case has been dismissed, and all claims return to both parties. But don't bring this case back to me," he added to McKenzie. "I'm not interested."

She grinned, gathering her papers. "Sounds good to me, your honor."

Surprisingly, Khoi had remained calm during the entire proceeding and answered every question factually. But now that the ordeal was over, a look of pure relief spread across his face, and he threw his back and said enthusiastically, "You did it! You really did it."

Somehow, McKenzie had been able to hold in her scream of delight until she was able to gather her papers into her briefcase and exit the courtroom into the hall. Standing in front of him, McKenzie had the sudden urge to hug him. She took a step forward as she smelled his familiar cologne again. Her heart pounded eagerly wanting to celebrate with Khoi. Opening her mouth to find something to say, McKenzie hesitated.

But Khoi didn't hesitate and took a bold step forward, wrapped her in his arms, and pulled her into a kiss.

Yes! She'd yearned to kiss him for days. McKenzie had done her best to ignore the growing desire, but this strong-willed man had wiggled his way into her life and her heart. He was passionate, and his confidence made her weak in the knees. She wrapped her arms around his neck as she entwined her fingers in his dark hair, pulling him closer.

His lips tasted like mints, and the way he ran his fingers down her spine sent shivers running throughout her entire body.

Pulling back slightly, McKenzie whispered, "It's about time."

Khoi smiled that crooked grin. "I was trying to be polite," he explained himself between quick kisses to her cheeks, eyelids, and nose.

She giggled, tugging him around the corner and into an empty courtroom. The small room was dimly lit, and not a soul was in sight as the door closed behind them. She's wanted to get out of the hallway so people wouldn't bump into them. Strangers could be so rude in the courthouse. "Liar. You just wanted me to handle your case first."

He backed her up against the nearest wall and pulled her back into his embrace. Face to face, his lips grinned against hers. "Maybe. Maybe not." Then he brushed his hands across her face. "Now, you really need to help me finish getting divorced."

She shook her head. "To avoid any further conflicts of interest, I'll refer you to the second-best lawyer in town, after me of course? One week tops." She smiled.

"Then, you really can't kick me out until Monday."

She chuckled. "Just shut up and kiss me," she instructed, not interested in talking anymore. They'd done plenty of that over the last couple of weeks, but not enough kissing. She dropped her bag beside them and tugged him closer. After all the drama she had this last month, she deserved this.

His lips were soft and warm, and his quiet moans were like music to her ears. With his body weight pressing her back against the wall, she lifted a leg and pressed it against his hip in an attempt to get closer to him in every way.

He sucked in a breath and deepened the kiss as all politeness went out the window, and every ounce of need coursed through his veins. "God, you are so beautiful. I've imagined you in my arms so many times, but my dreams were never as good as this."

Tangled in his embrace, her worries melted away the more he devoured her mouth, neck, and chin with his lips and tongue. His hands were gripping and squeezing her hips and back. And when he grabbed the back of her neck then pulled her head to the side to suck on her sensitive skin, she could feel her heart thumping loudly in her chest. Divorce law definitely had its perks, McKenzie told herself. Maybe this really was the best line of work for her.

THE END

THE ART OF FLOWERS

SHORT AND SWEET INTERRACIAL ROMANCE

CHAPTER 1

It's one in the afternoon, and the flower shop opened five hours ago. They had served several customers, and the workday was in full swing, but Jinan couldn't concentrate knowing that a certain beautiful gallery manager was just across the street.

Amber.

Amber was the most beautiful woman he'd ever laid eyes on. His heart skipped a beat every time she looked his way. Everything about her made him stand up and pay attention. From the sway of her curvy hips when she crossed a room to the musical sound of her laugh. She was like the freshest air that he was dying to inhale. Her skin was the color of a rich deep espresso, and her bright smile lit up the sky. Her natural hair was a beautiful halo of short tight curls. The sight of her took his breath away. The only problem was that she didn't know how he felt. He preferred to keep it a perfect secret, hiding behind a friendly smile.

He shook his head from side to side. He had to stop thinking about Amber, at least during work hours.

Jinan's flower delivery hasn't arrived yet, and he's pacing back and forth so frantically that his business partner Mike has pointed out to watch for wear in the floor several times.

It doesn't get any funnier the more he says it.

"Mike, where is it?" Jinan asks, peering out the window at every vehicle that drives past in hopes of spotting the delivery van.

"I don't know, Jinan. I don't see why you're so stressed. We have enough flowers to carry us for at least today, so even if it doesn't arrive today, we'll be fine," Mike says, pinching the bridge of his nose. Jinan is very aware that he's distressing the other man considerably.

"No, it needs to be today," Jinan says, turning on his heels to start pacing yet again. Mike sighs behind him and stands, ruffling his hair.

"Alright. I'm going out to do this delivery now. Just don't cause chaos because you're impatient," he says before disappearing out through the back door. Jinan scowls at his retreating back and moves over to the front desk, forcing himself to sit at it instead of pacing. Sighing, he starts to get to work making new displays for the front window, focusing on the delicate stems and blooms instead of the rising stress in his chest.

Thankfully, he manages to lose himself in the steady, soothing work for an hour or so and, finally, at two fifteen, the delivery van bound for their store appears. Jinan is on his feet in seconds, throwing the door open to help the driver carry the crates in carefully.

"Thanks a lot," he says distractedly as he gets to work, moving everything into the back storage room. Once all the crates are safely put away, Jinan rocks back onto his haunches and surveys his delivery, looking for what he needs. It takes him a few moments to spot the exact bloom he wants, but when he does, he carefully leans forward and plucks four of the flowers from their water.

With the flowers held delicately in one hand, he hurries back through to the front desk, rifling through the array of meticulously organized ribbons. Eventually, he finds a length of plain twine that he winds around the stems, tying it off into a clean, neat knot. He settles the miniature bouquet back into a bucket of water for the time being and waits for Mike to return.

As soon as he does, the pair of them get to work, making sure the shop is in perfect running order, with Mike prepping the deliveries for the next day while Jinan mans the front desk. Sundays are always a busy day for them, and Jinan's thankful for it today. It gives him something to think about other than the dark-haired woman just across the street. He actively pushes away all thoughts of Amber as he works, focusing instead on arranging pre-determined bouquets, on carefully writing out labels and notes to attach, on taking stock.

Around ten minutes before closing, a teenage boy wanders in - young and looking dazed and uncomfortable. Jinan glances up and offers a gentle smile. "Hi. Can I help you with anything?"

"Hi. I'm not really sure what I'm looking for. It's my girlfriend's birthday tomorrow, and I wanted to get her flowers, but I don't want anything really extravagant. I don't really know where to start," the boy says nervously, and Jinan smiles.

"I can help you with that. What's her favorite color?" Jinan asks, standing up and dusting his hands down. This is quite possibly the best part of his job - getting a chance to work with the customer to create something perfect.

"Purple. She loves purple," the boy says immediately, and Jinan grins in response.

"We can work with purple. Follow me. How about these lilac freesias?" he asks, gesturing to a small collection of flowers, and the boy smiles.

"They're nice. Would we put anything else in?" he says, reaching forward to brush his fingers across the petals.

"We can... I could make something small. It would be more of a posy than a bouquet really, but it would be nice and subtle enough to sit in her room without being overpowering," he says. "I'll do it now if you'd like that."

"That would be great. Also, do you know how much it'll be?" the boy asks, and Jinan knows that's been the source of his anxiety. Shrugging, he picks up some more blooms.

"Normally these arrangements are a little bit more but, because it's rare that I see someone so young who cares so much about their girlfriend, I'll give it to you for half price, does that sound good?" he says, watching the way his face lights up immediately.

"Oh, you don't have to do that!" the boy insists, and he shakes his head.

"Don't worry about it. You saved me from boredom," he says, trimming the excess foliage off some of the flowers and carefully arranging them into a provisional set up. "What do we think?" he asks, and the boy surveys the bouquet.

"Can we have a few more of the other purple ones?" he asks, and Jinan nods, gathering a few more lilac September flowers to thread through the bouquet.

"Better?" he asks, and the boy grins in response, nodding.

"It's perfect. Thank you so, so much. She's going to love them," he says. Jinan grins and carefully ties the stems together with a fine, white ribbon. He rings up the bouquet, applying the discount as he had promised. The boy pays quickly, thanking him profusely, and Jinan waves it off again.

"I hope she has a good birthday!" he calls as the boy leaves, and he smiles back gratefully. He carefully takes the time to clean up the trimmings from his workspace before checking the time. "Mike, are we ready to close up?" he calls into the back room.

"Yes, we're ready. I've prepared everything for tomorrow. I'm ready to close if you are," Mike replies, coming out of the room. "Are you okay to lock up if I duck out now? Lydia and I are going for dinner."

Jinan smiles fondly at Mike, who's beaming at the thought of his girlfriend and shoos him away. "Go on then, don't say I'm not good to you. Enjoy your date."

"Oh, I will," Mike calls back as he hurries out of the store.

Jinan sighs, with an amused smile playing around his lips, as he gets to work sweeping up the floor.

There is a quick rap at the door, and Jinan glances up, ready to give the usual spiel about being closed, when he sees Amber standing there, a shy smile curving her lips. He takes a moment to move.

He had spent all day trying not to think about her, and now she's standing outside his shop, looking radiant. Eventually, he shakes himself into movement and props the broom up against the wall as he unlocks the door to let her in.

"Amber. Hello," he says.

"Hi. I was just closing up and saw your lights were all still on. I wondered if you needed a hand with closing. Lydia and I managed to close up soon, so I was just about to head home," she says as she steps in carefully, caramel-eyed gaze sliding across all the flowers fondly.

"I just sent Mike home so he'd make his date," Jinan laughs. "I think I'm alright, but the company would be nice if you're not in a rush to get home," he says cautiously.

He doesn't need to worry. Amber nods immediately and saunters around the front desk to drop into his seat. "What do you think? Am I in the wrong business?" she asks, an amused glint dancing in her eyes.

Jinan smiles at her, this beautiful woman smirking slyly while sat surrounded by delicate, soft blooms.

"If you ever get bored of the gallery, I'd welcome you in an instant," he says warmly, watching as her smirk slips into a soft, pleasant smile instead.

"Good to know," she murmurs.

Jinan remembers with a start just what he should be doing at the moment and quickly hurries over to the back room. "I have beers back here if you want one?" he offers, hand trembling as he reaches for the handle.

"Sounds great, thanks. I can't stay too late, so just one for me, please."

"No worries, early start for me tomorrow too," he says, ducking into the back to grab two of the beers from where he and Mike store them. Sometimes after a late closing, he and Mike would share a drink before heading home. Less so these days since Mike usually headed home to be with his girlfriend, Lydia. After a moment's hesitation, he picks up the little bouquet of tiger lilies.

He sets the opened beer next to her and, when she looks up to give him yet another brilliant smile, he offers the bouquet across the table. "I ordered these in as a gift - just to say welcome, now that we're neighbors – or at least the gallery and store are," he says.

"Oh Jinan, you really didn't have to," she says softly, although she's gazing at the orange blooms in wonder. "They're beautiful."

"Don't worry about it. I just wanted to say thanks," he says bashfully before cracking his own beer open and asking her quietly about her day. She tears her gaze from the flowers and launches into the story of her latest customer who had come in for a small painting but fallen in love with a ridiculously expensive one.

Jinan thinks it sounds like love.

They nurse their beers for a good few hours, chatting away aimlessly but never once losing the flow of conversation. Amber's halfway through telling Jinan about her sister's job out of state when the flowers to her right catch her eye again, and she sighs.

"What flowers are these?" She asks, reaching out to touch a petal lightly.

"They're tiger lilies. One of my favorites but not always popular, so we never order too many," he explains, and Amber softens.

"I don't see why they're not popular. They're beautiful. Do these ones have a meaning?"

Jinan freezes momentarily before clearing his throat. "They signify gratitude..." he trails off awkwardly, praying that she buys the lie. She hums thoughtfully before returning to her story, and he exhales a sigh of relief, ruffling his hair as he lets himself listen to her soothing voice once more.

It isn't until another hour or two later, when she's said her goodbyes and gathered her things and hugged him warmly, that he lets himself ruminate on the true meaning. Sighing, Jinan leans his back heavily against the door, gazing at where she had been sitting for so long.

"The tiger lily means *I dare you to love me*," he whispers into the silence.

He flicks the lights off and heads out of the door.

Monday morning dawns bright and clear, and it's freezing cold outside. Jinan glares pointedly at the temperature reading in his car as he sets off towards the shop, in the hopes that Mike has already gotten there and started opening up. Of course, that is like asking for a miracle and, as he pulls up to the storefront, his phone starts to ring insistently. Mike's name and picture flash up, and Jinan sighs slowly, dreading what awaits him.

"Jinan, I'm so sorry, but Julia's gone into labor, and I really want to be there, is it okay if I take today off?" Mike asks, his voice is frantic.

"Oh god, yes, of course. Send your sister my love," Jinan says without a second thought. "I'll manage just fine without you for the next few days," he assures him.

Mike says a hurried thank you and hangs up. Jinan sighs and steels himself for a busy day now that he will be manning the place alone. He strolls over to the door and pats his pockets down for the keys.

He freezes and then pats them down again.

"Oh damn it," he mutters, realizing that he must have left them inside last night. The shutters had locked down behind him automatically as they usually did. "Okay," he says to himself, stepping back and rocking back and forth on his heels. "Locksmith. Call him," he says after a moment, pulling his phone out and finding a number for a local locksmith.

He paces back and forth as he speaks, eventually working out that the earliest they can get to him is two in the afternoon. He accepts and thanks them before hanging up and leaning heavily against the wall. This is exactly what he didn't need today. He's about to climb back in his car and head home when a familiar dark head pops out of the gallery across the road.

"Jinan! Are you alright?" Amber calls, beckoning him over.

Jinan smiles warmly at her, despite the frustration surging through him as he crosses the road to her place. "I'm fine, but I managed to lock myself out of the shop. Mike's rushed home because his sister's gone into labor, and the earliest the locksmith can get to me is two," he huffs out all in a rush, and Amber's eyes widen.

"That sounds like one hell of a morning. I'm afraid that locksmithing isn't one of my hidden talents, but I have sodas in here and granola bars, and it's somewhere warm to sit while you wait if you want," she offers, opening the door wider.

Jinan nods gratefully. "That would be perfect, Amber, thanks."

As he passes by, he catches a hint of her floral perfume. She smells like a moonlit stroll through a lush garden blend of fresh jasmine, blue violets, sheer lavender, and soft musk.

"No problem. I have a couple of prospective buyers coming in, but you're more than welcome to sit and look at the paintings," she says softly as they step into the space.

He nods and sits on the modern white sofa that Amber points out to him. "Do you want a soda?" She asks.

"Yes, thank you," he says, raising his hand in greeting as Lydia wanders past.

Kuaba Gallery was a beautiful contemporary space featuring paintings, sculptures, and other works by international artists of color and local African American artists. Jinan looked around at the various white walls that seemed to disappear seamlessly into the charcoal black industrial ceiling. The floor to ceiling windows that lined the front of the gallery ushered in rays of sunlight to flood the open space. Nine-foot art display cubes were strategically placed throughout the airy exhibition room, creating a wonder-inspiring maze of artwork. He could get lost for days in its beauty.

"What are you doing here, Casanova?" A tall blonde dressed in all white asks breezily, and Jinan grunts in annoyance at the nickname. It's Mike's girlfriend, Lydia. She is pretty but very direct when it comes to conversations. She and Mike have been dating for several months now, and things seem to be going very well.

"Locked myself out of the shop, locksmith won't arrive until two and Mike's sis..."

"...sister is in labor, yes," Lydia finishes for him, waving her hand. "I know, I know. Are you here to learn a little art appreciation? Maybe some restoration classes?" She smiles jokingly.

Jinan returns the smile, then something more intriguing catches his eye. "No, thanks. I'll just watch Trish," he says, and Lydia's eyebrows lift at the new nickname. Thankfully, she says nothing and swans off, calling for Cara so that they can go over paperwork.

Amber returns moments later with a soda in one hand. "Here we go. We keep a case in the staff room fridge in case a client needs a drink, but we won't miss one," she laughs as she passes it to him. He grins back and cracks it open.

"Thanks, Amber, you're the best," he says. She blushes slightly at the compliment, and he watches the rose-pink flush spread across her cheeks with a curious interest. It makes her look all the more beautiful. He's about to say so when a voice breaks their moment.

"Amber, the client is here!"

Amber shoots him an apologetic smile and turns to get to work charming the man who already seems more smitten with her than with the painting.

The meeting takes a little over an hour, and Jinan watches Amber diligently for the whole time, studying the way her brow furrows, the way she pauses every so often to fix her smile. The time flies by as he watches every little quirk of her at work.

She's barely closed the deal - the man is still paying in the office - when Lydia gestures for her, nodding to another buyer who walked in off the street.

The majority of the afternoon carries on similarly. It's obvious that Amber and Lydia have built a fairly steady flow of customers up and, even though it means he doesn't get to talk to her as much as he'd like, he can't help but be proud of her as he watches her navigate the day with ease.

He's just settled down to watch her do her second negotiation of the day, which happens to be the young woman, Rachel, when the receptionist Cara flops down on the sofa next to him, looking at him curiously. "Lydia's right then," she says, and he startles.

"I have no idea what you mean," he says, although he's well aware of the fact that he's tried to cover his nervousness up far too quickly for it to be believable.

"Yes, you do. Lydia's told me all about how she thinks you're in love with Amber. I didn't know whether to believe it or not, but the way you look at her when she isn't watching..." She trails off, and Jinan groans, scrubbing a hand over his face. Cara shrugs. "You're not the most subtle person, Jinan, but I think you probably have a chance with her," she admits.

Jinan is about to ask more about that particular revelation, but Cara just plows on. "But that's the problem. Ask Lydia - she and I adore Amber so much, but historically, her taste in boyfriends is awful. So I suppose what I'm saying is that you seem really nice and I think she would be really happy with you. However, if you hurt her, you'll have Lydia and me to deal with, and her sister probably and even I'm scared of her."

Overwhelmed with that information, Jinan blinks at her for a few moments before shaking his head. "I'd never dream of hurting her."

"I figured as much, but I wanted to make sure," Cara says with a soft smile. "And don't ask about how she feels - it's not my place. You'll have to pluck up the courage to ask her," she adds, and Jinan huffs.

"Fine," he sighs, deciding to drop the subject. "How did you meet Amber?" He asks instead, tilting his head in interest.

"I was an unemployed fine arts major," Cara explains. "Amber sold one of the paintings for me even though it wasn't very good. She gave me a chance. I really liked her, so I kept up with what she was doing. I didn't really intend on becoming a receptionist, but when I found out she and Lydia had set up this gallery, I asked if she was hiring. I was lucky because she said yes," Cara smiles warmly at the memory and shrugs. "She's been good to me - she's always been patient with me. Lydia, too. We're protective of our little group," she shrugs.

"I know," he says quietly.

"I think you'd be good for Amber, and I like you. She's agreed to throw a party for my birthday this weekend at her house. Why don't you come along? No doubt Lydia will want to bring Mike, and I was going to invite my boyfriend as well. At least you'd get a chance to talk casually without work in the way," she offers.

Jinan grins at her and nods once. "Sounds perfect, Cara. Thank you."

Cara grins back, open and friendly now that she's said what was on her mind. "You'll probably just get teased by Lydia all night, so maybe don't thank me yet." With that, she stands and disappears back to her seat at the reception.

The locksmith calls ten minutes later to say he's outside. Jinan waves goodbye to Amber, who gives him a brilliant smile in return, and he strolls over to his own store, feeling lighter than he has in days. Perhaps he really does have a chance.

Friday night rolls around, and Jinan finds himself tapping his foot anxiously as he waits for Mike to show up. The two of them have agreed to take a cab to Amber's together, and Jinan has never been more impatient to get anywhere in his life. He's changed outfits twice already and made sure his hair is just perfectly set before resorting to restlessly wandering around his apartment. Eventually, there's a sharp knock at the door, and Jinan practically flies to open it. Mike blinks at him in surprise. "Cab's waiting."

"Great. Let's go."

"Jinan, you have to settle down before we get there, or you're going to scare Amber off," Mike says, chuckling lightly. Jinan flips him off before climbing into the car.

The drive doesn't take long, and soon, Jinan and Mike are approaching the correct apartment. Mike knocks lightly and the door swings open to reveal Amber, smiling brightly and clutching a drink in one hand. While she and Mike greet each other, Jinan takes a moment to take her in, everything from the long dark curls, the loose tank top, and the dark denim cut-offs. She looks ravishing. He manages to flash her a bright smile and doesn't spontaneously collapse when she tugs him into a warm hug of greeting. He counts that as a win. "Come on in! The girls are here already and-"

"Amber! Hey, get in here, we want to do shots," Lydia calls from the sitting room, and Amber shrugs helplessly.

"Come with me. You can put your things in the kitchen," she says. The boys trail after her and wave their hellos to Lydia and Cara, who are sitting with three shots of whiskey poured out. Amber picks up one, clinks her glass with the other two, and knocks the golden liquid back with ease. "Right, this way," she says, turning towards the kitchen.

"That was impressive," Jinan says, and Amber laughs brightly as she steps into the kitchen and gestures for them to set their contribution to the party on the white counters, which are mostly empty, save for several bottles of alcohol.

"Not particularly. I've spent almost all of my twenties with Lydia. You can't do that without learning how to deal with shots," she says, pulling two glasses down from a cupboard and passing them over. Jinan laughs and pours himself a generous measure of whiskey before adding a mixer. He passes both bottles to Mike, who does the same.

"Maybe I'll challenge her to a competition. I used to be decent at shots back in my day," Jinan grins, and Amber shakes her head, a fond smile curling her rose-pink lips.

"On your own head, be it," she says in a sing-song voice before breezing through to join the girls.

Jinan grimaces as he downs the shot, shaking his head in disbelief. "Lydia, I have no idea how you do it," he hisses, slamming the shot glass down next to her empty one. She and Jinan have been going shot for shot on tequila for about five minutes, and he resigns himself to tapping out.

"Practice, Casanova," she grins.

Jinan rolls his eyes and sits back, his gaze drifting across the room in search for Amber. When he doesn't spot her, he sighs and pushes himself to his feet, trying not to think about how the room lurches dangerously as he does so. Carefully, he makes his way into the kitchen, trying not to look as tipsy as he feels.

Sure enough, Amber is perching on her kitchen counter, legs tucked under her as she scrolls through her phone with one hand and sips at her rum and coke with the other.

"Hey," he murmurs, grabbing a chair facing her and sinking into it quickly, slanting a warm smile at her.

"Hey. I thought you were in a shot competition with Lydia?" she asks with a tilt of her head.

"I was. *Was* being the operative word." He laughs. "I have no idea how she can drink like that."

"Practice," Amber quips immediately, locking her phone and setting it aside.

"That's exactly what she said," he huffs, shaking his head disbelievingly. "Why are you hiding away in here anyway?" Jinan asks softly.

"No reason - sometimes I just like to have a moment somewhere quiet before I go back to the party," she says. He scans her face carefully for any sign of something being wrong but finds absolutely nothing to indicate that so he merely shrugs.

"That's fair. I can go if you want," he offers, moving to stand, although he stops as soon as she shakes her head.

"Don't worry about it," she smiles kindly, shifting slightly on the counter. As she does so, the tiny piece of black ink on the inside of her ankle catches his eye, and he nods his head towards it.

"Was that your first tattoo?" he asks, and she smiles, glancing down at her ankle.

"Yes, when I was nineteen. My mother hated it, but she came around eventually," Amber grins, tracing the silhouette of the ballerina that adorns her skin.

"Any reason you chose a ballerina?" Jinan asks curiously, shifting fractionally closer to peer at the detailed ink.

Amber inhales sharply, and he grimaces, wondering if he had hit upon a sore spot. "Sorry, I shouldn't have asked..."

"No, it's fine. I just haven't told this story in a while," she says, pushing dark curls from her face before letting out a slow breath. "I used to dance as a kid. I danced a lot, in fact, and I was good. The National Ballet School invited me to join them when I was nine. So I did, and there was a real possibility of me becoming one of the principals by the time I was seventeen or so, but there was an issue with my ankles. Overuse injury. I had surgery, but the strain of being en pointe after that was too much for my shins, so I was forced to retire. So I got the tattoo as a tribute to that part of my life," she says.

"Oh, Amber, I'm so sorry," he murmurs. With that knowledge, Jinan glances back at her tattoo and is able to pick out the neat surgical scars on her legs, faded over the years but still visible. "I shouldn't have asked, I'm sorry."

"It's fine. I'm incredibly happy with the gallery and, if I had been in ballet, I would never have gotten a chance to know Lydia better or met Cara. Or have met you. So really, there's a silver lining. Besides, I love all my tattoos, and I wouldn't have been able to get them if I was a ballet dancer," she grins, a little lighter now.

Or have met you. Aware of the fact that she's obviously trying to change the subject, Jinan smiles and goes along with it. "How many do you have? I think I've only seen two," he says.

"I have five," she answers with a soft smile. "I have the one on my shoulder that matches Lydia's, I have the ballerina, I've got one on my hip, one on my thigh and one on my sternum," she says, counting them all off. Jinan smiles at her, even as his mind starts to whirl with thoughts as to what sort of ink she has hidden away.

"Oh? What are the others?" he asks, praying that his voice stays level.

"I have a quote on my hip, I have a music staff on my thigh and a floral piece here on my sternum," she explains, reaching up to trace just under the curve of her breasts. He swallows hard and forces himself not to stare.

"They sound pretty," he manages. She smiles and shuffles closer until her legs are either side of him, and his face is level with her stomach. Carefully, she twists slightly to the side and pulls the hem of her tank top up to reveal a neatly printed quote across the milk chocolate of her hip, reading simply *'in movement there is life,'* and he exhales quietly, letting the words on her skin sink into his mind.

"It's beautiful," he says softly. "Where is it from?"

"It's by Alan Cohen. The whole sentence reads; *There is more security in the adventurous and exciting, for in movement there is life, and in change there is power,*" she recites it with ease and shrugs one shoulder. "It's encouraging."

"It's beautiful," he says, at a loss for words still as he forcibly tears his gaze away from the sliver of exposed skin. She smiles in response and slides forward a little on the counter to push her denim cut-offs up so he can see the music staff tattoo that wraps around her upper thigh.

"That must have taken a long time," he says, mouth suddenly dry, as he fights the urge to reach out and trace the lines making up the staff.

"A few hours," she answers, pitching her voice just as low as his. Then she says the words that leave him reeling. "You can touch it, Jinan. I can tell you want to," she whispers. He snaps his gaze up to her and finds nothing but surety in her eyes. Shaking only slightly, Jinan sets his beer next to her and carefully lifts his hand to settle on the skin of her thigh, cool and smooth under his hand as his fingers dance lightly across the ink. He watches in interest as goosebumps rise in the wake of his touch. Unbidden, Cara's confession that Amber is interested in him too floats to the front of his mind, and he looks up at Amber where she sits above him on the counter.

Slowly, as though testing the waters, Jinan stands to put himself at the same height as her, although his hand never leaves her thigh, his thumb still tracing back and forth across her porcelain skin. "Amber. Tell me to stop if you want me to," he whispers.

"Don't stop," she breathes out and, reassured, Jinan brings his free hand up to cup her jaw and dips his head to hers, pressing their lips together. He's never been one to believe in the cliché of fireworks happening when you kiss someone, but what he does know is that kissing Amber might be more intoxicating than any spirit he's ever drunk in his life.

She lets out a soft, breathy whimper against his lips, and it's nearly his undoing. Eventually, he pulls back, taking in the soft fluttering of her lashes and the swelling to her lips. She looks beautiful. He tells her so, and she laughs, wry and breathless, before reaching up to swipe her thumb across his bottom lip to remove traces of her lipstick.

"Jinan," she starts, voice husky and rough, "will you stay?" she finishes, a smirk painting her lips.

He groans at her sudden brazenness.

"Let's wait till everyone leaves," Amber murmurs, hopping down from the counter and disappearing into the living room. Jinan exhales heavily and spends a moment trying to get himself under control and turns to head back out to the living area.

The rest of the party flies by, and no one mentions their encounter in the kitchen, although Jinan is positive that Cara and Lydia suspect that something.

Once everyone has said their goodbyes, Amber closes the door behind her and turns to Jinan. "I'm trusting my heart. I hope it's right," she whispers as they meet each other in the center of the room.

Jinan takes Amber's face into his hands. He can't help but caress her cheeks with his thumbs. He speaks slowly, just enough to let her know exactly how he feels. "I'm in love with you, and I've been in love with you for quite some time."

He watches as her eyes grow wide in response to his declaration. His thumbs gradually make their way to her lips and gently stroke them. She leans forward to pull him in close, and he presses his forehead against hers. They gaze into each other's eyes. Breathing in deeply with their mouths so close.

"Please let me love you," he whispers. "Please."

Before she has a chance to respond, Jinan places his lips on hers. The touch is so soft and gentle as their kiss starts off slow. Each is wanting to remember this moment of them coming together. Amber's eyes remain open for a few seconds longer than his, just so she can see the passion written across his face. All at once, Amber's other senses come alive. Her eyes flutter shut, and she loses herself in the sweetness of his lips. He tastes delicious, like caramel and vanilla ice cream. Mmm, so good.

A low deep sound reverberates through her ears, and she realizes that it is coming from her. The kiss grows more hungry. He moves in closer and pulls lightly on her hair as he deepens their kiss even more. It's when Amber opens her mouth that she hears him for the first time, a deep throaty moan. His mouth moves away from her lips and follows her jawline. With a sideways tilt of her head, he devours her exposed throat with a sense of urgency and need. Jinan is determined to taste every part of her.

And throughout the night, that is exactly what he does.

THE END

FOREVER AHEAD OF US

SHORT & SWEET INTERRACIAL ROMANCE

BY

JADE MOON

CHAPTER ONE

Kenya was so in love that she felt blessed and afraid at the same time. Like many other women, she had experienced her share heartache and heartbreak in the past, but she survived. As a matter of fact, she grew and flourished. Now, she was in her last year of law school and in a very healthy relationship with her fiancé, Dasan.

He was kind and considerate. He respected her opinions, just like she respected his quiet nature. After meeting his parents, she understood the laid back part of his personality more. Both his parents were born and raised in China but had decided to stay in California after graduating from Stanford University. Her parents had also graduated from Stanford, so it almost seemed like fate when the two legacies met at the same university and fell in love.

It had been four years, and she fell more in love with him each day. Either she was at his place, or he was at hers. The couple couldn't bear to sleep apart from each other. So it was no coincidence that when Kenya woke up each morning, her eyes were drawn to the silver glint on her hand. *Engaged*, she thought, *Dasan and I are engaged.*

He had given her the ring almost two years ago. However, he was not the kind of man to pressure her to give him an immediate answer, so days had turned into weeks and months, and finally, years.

She hid the ring like a secret wherever she went out. If they were in public, the ring was slid into a pocket or a purse or simply left behind in her jewelry box. It felt too unnerving having people glance at it, even if it was just a casual glance with no pressure intended.

She loved him, she did, but she had taken too long to give him her 'yes,' and now she didn't know how to bring it up again. Even the week they had just spent at her parents' lake house hadn't given her a chance to slip in her answer.

Besides, she had forgotten to bring the ring with her, so it felt odd bringing it up then.

The couple had met during their junior and senior year in college. He was one year older, but they both had set their sights on law school. She had dreamed of working in environmental law since she was a child, and he was equally passionate about a career in international relations. Life was good. They got along great, communicated well, and had a lot of things in common. In addition to being equally driven and focused, they were also very private about their personal lives. Dasan respected Kenya's desire to finish her law degree and pass the bar exam before marriage, and she appreciated his understanding nature.

She pulled into her parking spot at their apartment building, and he got out of the car before she even shut off the engine. He went to the trunk and grabbed both their suitcases, but thankfully waited for her to get out of the car and didn't walk away without her. She shouldn't have been so relieved at such a little thing, like him waiting for her, but she was. He followed her up and into the apartment. While he carried their bags directly into their bedroom, she took off her shoes and immediately went to the drawer in the little hall table.

It was by far the longest she had been without her ring in the last two years. She didn't wear it out, so she took it off every day. But normally she got to put it back on every evening when they came home. If they had switched apartments from his to hers or vice versa that night, she always made a quick stop to pick it up. She even wore it at night while they slept just so she could have a few more hours with it to make up for all the hours she went without.

So she took a moment to take it in before she put it on. She knew every line, every detail, but it felt like forever since she had seen it. It was almost like the first night he gave it to her all over as she examined it. When she slipped it back on her finger, her hand finally felt whole again.

Dasan stepped into the hallway and watched Kenya place the ring reverently back on her finger. He stared as he saw her eyes light up with pleasure as she glanced up into the hall mirror and placed her hand on her shoulder, so she could look at the ring near her face in the frame. The glint of the diamond looked perfect against her caramel brown skin. Then she brought her hand up closer to her face. He had always known that the ring complimented her full cheeks and large doe eyes divinely. She was as beautiful to him as the day they first met.

Finally, she glanced deeper into the mirror's reflection and saw Dasan standing behind her in the mirror. He was watching her with inexplicably sad eyes. Not allowing herself to overthink it, she closed the distance between them and threw her arms around his neck. He responded immediately, arms holding her tight against him.

"Can you please just hold me for a few minutes before we have whatever fight we're about to have? Just like this."

"Kenya," he whispered.

She already felt better. It was the softest tone she had heard out of him in over a week. She melted into him. Her hands tangled in his hair as she nuzzled her face into his neck.

He drew in a deep breath as he caressed her back, neck, and hips in a way he hadn't been able to in a week. Their breathing synced, and they relaxed in each other's' arms.

I missed this.

Me too.

When they finally broke apart, they ended up at the dining room table, which was designated as neutral territory for their serious discussions. Kenya refused to let go of his hand, keeping their linked fingers in full view sitting on top of the table between them.

"I think you should go first," she said. "I'm sorry that I asked you to cut back on the affection while we were at my parents' house, but I'm sure there is more going on here than that. I feel at a loss because I really don't know what it is."

"Yes." He ran his unoccupied hand across his face, unsure how to begin. "Yes. I'm sorry. There was that. But it was more. I love you..."

Kenya tried to cut in and reaffirm the same, but he shook his head to cut her off.

"I know you love me. But somehow, it just felt like we had gone back in time. Before us. Not the us from the past two years. Not being able to touch you for the past week, it felt like those first years all over again. I know you're not ready to get married, and you didn't want your parents asking about it, and that's why you wanted us to tone things down. But I ended up feeling like one day I'm going to wake up and you won't be there, and it will all be over. I had to wake up without you because you insisted on separate bedrooms while we were there. I missed you terribly, even though we were in the same house. I couldn't hold you or kiss you, and I felt like I was losing you. The feeling got worse every day." He held up a hand. "That's not your fault, I know. I shut down. I got completely wrapped up in my own head and couldn't get out of it. I'm sorry."

Kenya had no idea what to say. She had known something bigger was wrong but had no idea it was that big. That he questioned their relationship and her commitment to it, even if he recognized that those thoughts were based on old insecurities and not their current life. She needed to process, to think before she responded. She needed more information.

"And how are you feeling now?" She wasn't sure the answer was going to be good, but she needed to know.

"When I saw the look on your face when you put your ring back on, I felt relieved. More so, when you hugged me. I feet the emptiness seeping away just from you holding my hand now. I love you so much, and I guess I just need to physically know that you're with me, and somehow, everything is okay."

"But I can't always be holding you, Dasan." She clasped her other hand over their joined hands to emphasize this was not one of those moments. "I'll be with you forever, but there are going to be times that we can't be physically together. So we need a plan because I don't think I can handle it if you check out on me again. It's been so lonely and wretched for me too. Not even just the sleeping apart for a week, but not talking like we always do. I need you, too, and I don't want you to feel like that either. I never even guessed you were carrying all that around."

"I should have talked to you. It was a mistake, though I didn't want to ruin your visit with your parents. This was just a setback, I'm sure, but it's going to be okay." He calmly stroked her hair. "I know I have you. I know taking your time with the next step is important to you. It is to me too."

"We need a plan," she reiterated. "What helps you the most? What can I do?"

"You don't need to do anything special. Just holding you, talking with you. It's all I need. That and time. As much time as I can get with you."

Kenya's brain raced, taking in what he was saying and pairing it up with what she had been considering for months.

"So my ring helps, right? When you gave it to me, you said it wasn't an engagement ring if I didn't want it to be. Well, what if I want it to be now?"

His mouth fell open before quickly breaking into a huge grin transforming his whole face with pure joy. She loved how his dark brown eyes dipped in the outer corners whenever he smiled.

"You want to get married?"

"Yes, I do."

Simultaneously, they both abandoned their chairs to come together in a kiss over the middle of the table.

For the first time in a week, she got to kiss him properly. *I missed you so much.* She held on to him by his shoulders and climbed up onto the table. Without breaking away from him, she crawled across so that more than just their lips could touch. *Closer.*

He swept her up into his arms, bridal style, and looked down at her. "We're getting married?"

"We're getting married," she affirmed. She stretched up to kiss him, but it didn't seem close enough. Dasan had the same thought and started walking, carrying her to their bedroom.

An hour later, Dasan sat up against their pillows while she lay at his side. Her head rested on his chest, allowing her to feel his heartbeat. She lazily traced swirls over his stomach, luxuriating in the ability to run her hands over him again as much as she wanted after such a long drought. He kept hold of her left hand, slowly kissing every inch of it, but paying particular attention to her ring finger.

"We got distracted before we could finish making a plan," she said.

He ran a finger down her neck, trailing it down her chest. "The best kind of distraction," he said smiling.

She hummed in agreement. "It's a good thing that I already have a plan in mind."

"You do?"

"So we're getting married and..."

"We are getting married," he cut her off, reiterating her words with such a tone of awe. She could feel his smile.

"Yes, love. Wedding planning takes time."

"Right."

She could feel him nodding with his whole body.

"I'm studying for the bar exam in a few months, and you just got hired at the refugee non-profit, so we're just too busy to plan a wedding right now. Maybe we can just get through the next six months and let everything settle down. Then we announce our engagement to our families and start wedding planning. It will take at least a year for that."

"A year?"

"I swear. A year. But that leaves us with a fall wedding. What do you think?"

"I'd like it to be outdoors, so summer is probably better. I can wait."

"Can you? You would be willing to push out the date until a little over two years from now? It's technically a long engagement, but since we are already fully committed to forever, I'm not sure that matters."

"It's going to happen. It's okay if it takes a while, so we get it right."

"Good. Then when we tell our families this fall, I think I should just start wearing my ring all the time."

He leaned down to nuzzle his head against hers. "I can't believe we are getting married. I know we made our vows to each other two years ago, and we're already beyond just engaged, but still..."

She laughed, joyful from how happy he was. She was just as happy too. "I've been thinking about it for a while," she confesses. "I wanted to say yes, but I was afraid I had waited too long."

"I've been thinking about it every day for the past two years," he murmured into her shoulder. "All you had to do was say the word."

"And yet you never asked me about it again," she teased.

"My biggest mistake," he said. "I didn't want you to feel pressured."

"I know." The last two hours had fixed everything that had felt wrong over the past two years, but she wanted to make sure. "So we have a plan. Six more months and then we start wedding planning. We'll communicate better in the meantime. Is that going to be enough to give you what you need to feel secure in our commitment?"

"Yes, I can survive. Just six months until we announce the engagement."

She smiles.

"Can you please bring your ring with you when we visit my parents for Thanksgiving?" He brushed his fingers around the ring as he spoke. "Even if you keep your hands in your pockets half the time, I just like to see it. It's a reminder that you really plan to stay in my life."

"I was thinking the exact same thing. I can't go for a week without it again. My hand just feels wrong."

She gazed at their joined hands lying on top of her stomach. Everything was just as it should be in that moment. The exhaustion of everything was starting to hit her, and she let her eyes drift shut.

"We are finally going to take the next step, Kenya," he said softly.

She didn't know if he was talking about announcing their engagement or actually getting married. It didn't matter. To all of it, he was right.

"Yes, we really are."

CHAPTER TWO

Kenya stood in front of the full-length mirror and pulled the straps of her dress onto her shoulders. The evening weather was perfect, warm with a gentle breeze blowing through the air.

"Can you zip me up?"

She really didn't need Dasan to zip her up. It wasn't as if the dress was so constricting that she couldn't manage the zipper herself. But rather than cranking her arm around in its socket, it was much more pleasant to have him do it.

"Sure."

She admired him in the mirror as he came up behind her. He was just wearing shorts and a t-shirt. They weren't going anywhere particularly nice since it was his restaurant pick, which was why she had picked a simpler sundress instead of getting all dressed up. It was Dasan's favorite dress. Not that he had ever said that, but she noticed how terrible he was at tearing his gaze away from the cutouts whenever she wore it, so she assumed it could be counted as his favorite.

He gently swept all her hair over her shoulder, gently kissing the back of her now exposed neck. His fingers traced her spine all the way down until he reached the zipper. He zipped her up and then smoothed down her dress for good measure, gratuitously running over her every curve. He lingered on the open areas, his fingers brushing her exposed skin.

Yes, it was much better to have him help her get dressed.

"Thanks, love." She reached back and slid her hand around his arm, pushing his sleeve out of the way. "I just need my purse, and then I'm ready whenever you are."

"I'll go grab it for you," he said but didn't move. She didn't let go either, letting her fingers glide back and forth across his arm. His right hand came to rest on her hip, and she covered his hand with her own, intertwining their fingers. He met her eyes in the mirror and smiled back at her. Her ring twinkled in the light.

They took Kenya's car to dinner. She drove one-handed most of the way, glad that she drove an automatic so that she didn't need to let go of Dasan's hand. Parking was, as usual, a disaster, meaning they ended up on the street several blocks away from their destination. She had to wait until there was a break in traffic so she could get out and hurry off the road. He held out a hand for her while she stepped up onto the sidewalk. She took his hand but expected him to let go as soon as she was out of the street.

He didn't. Instead, his other hand quickly covered the top of her hand.

"Kenya, you forgot. The ring is still on."

"I didn't forget."

He searched her eyes, needing to understand.

"I know we don't do gifts, but this isn't exactly a gift."

"Oh, yes, it is."

His lips met hers, and she spared a quick thought for the mess her lipstick was about to be before she let herself get swept away in the moment. She restrained herself from latching onto his hair and settled for her arms around his neck. But she didn't resist or pull back when he deepened the kiss. She met him with equal passion, relieved that he was on board with her one-sided decision.

They'd planned it so they would arrive home exactly six months from the official start of their engagement. Kenya had called Dasan's mother and asked if she would be willing to throw a belated birthday party for him. She quickly agreed, and Kenya had her whole family added to the guest list. Nothing about that was particularly unusual since he insisted on including her family in all possible events. So they were sure their families didn't know about the announcement they planned to make.

When they parted for air, she nuzzled her nose against his. "Happy birthday, Dasan."

He kissed her again. Then his grip on her hips shifted, and instinct made her grab his shoulders just in time. He spun her around in the middle of the sidewalk. She automatically extended her legs and pointed her toes. It was like something out of a movie.

His whole face was lit up, and she was sure hers matched. With absolutely nothing holding her shoes onto her feet, first one and then the other flew off. Kenya gasped the moment the first shoe left her foot, and he caught on when her heel smacked against the brick storefront beside them.

She burst into a fit of giggles. Dasan placed her back on the ground and went to collect her shoes for her while she patiently waited in bare feet on the cement. He knelt down, and she let him pick up each foot and slide them back into her heels.

"Sorry, Kenya," he murmured.

Still laughing, she brushed her fingers through his black hair, tucking what she could behind his ear as he stood back up.

"It's fine," she assured him, giving him a quick kiss. But then she took in the sight of his mouth, with her lipstick all around it. She ran her thumb over the worst of it. "We do need to fix this, though."

She fished some tissues out of her purse, handing one to him and taking one for herself. She pulled out her compact mirror while Dasan used the reflection in her car window.

"I'm not used to having to worry about smudging lipstick in public anymore," she said. She tried to not ruin her foundation too much as she removed the wayward red marks around her mouth. "I'm going to have to switch to a lip stain."

Dasan straightened up as she began reapplying her lipstick. "I don't know what that is, but if it means more kissing, then I'm all for it."

"In general, yes. But let's go enjoy your birthday dinner right now."

He took her hand with her pinky between his index and middle fingers, but she was acutely aware of her ring pressed against the side of his finger. To the passersby, they were just another couple in love walking down the street. To her, the ring was the only thing she could think about. This was the first time she had worn her ring outside for all to see.

She really didn't think this could count as an appropriate proper birthday gift to him, given that this was really a gift to herself. To finally hold his hand and take him to dinner and sit in the booth and have his arm draped around her - knowing that she had given him her answer - that they were each other's more than ever. It was a gift to both of them.

After enjoying dinner together, the couple drove to his parent's house and knocked on the door. Kenya was glad that despite her small birthday surprise for Dasan, the plan for their families was still on track.

As soon as they walked into the house, Kenya didn't even get to take her shoes off before the ring was noticed. Then there was screaming and hugging and kissing, and it was another ten minutes before Kenya actually got her shoes off and could move away from the entranceway.

Dasan beamed with happiness as both their families celebrated their engagement.

"Should we show the ring to everyone now?" she asked. "It feels strange after stowing it away for so long. Like a breach of privacy, almost."

They were curled up on his couch, having a quiet night in.

"I'd love to scream it from the rooftops, but posting on our social media might be a saner choice."

"How do you want to do it then?"

Dasan looked at her quizzically. "You should know by now that I have no sense of what's appropriate when it comes to posting things on social media. How can I be marrying someone who knows me so little?"

She tried not to roll her eyes. "Yes, I'm so silly for thinking my fiancé might have an opinion about our engagement announcement."

He groaned. "Oh god, please can we not do anything as formal as an engagement announcement? That sounds like something for stuffy people."

"See, you do have an opinion," she elbowed him lightly. "How about posting a photo of us?"

"I don't really want to take one right now." He ruffled his hair and gestured down at his sweats.

"Fair enough. How about I just post a photo of my ring and tag you in it?"

"Is that a thing that people do?"

"Yes, love, it is."

"Whatever you think is best."

She sat up and looked around the room, looking for the best lighting. It was already dark outside, so natural light wasn't an option.

Dasan massaged her shoulders as she considered her options. She needed a backdrop of some sort. She didn't really want to post just a photo of her hand. Luckily, she had just painted her fingernails yesterday, so they weren't chipped yet.

"I think I know what I should do. Can you turn on all the lamps and lights?"

Dasan's TV hung above the fireplace on the wall, but Kenya had still tucked mementos on the corners of the mantel. She went to the bookcase and picked up the picture of them standing in the meadow behind her parents' home and set it on the mantel next to the bouquet of fresh flowers Dasan had got her as a surprise that morning. Holding up her hand next to them, she considered the arrangement. The flowers needed to be pulled a little more to the side.

Dasan came up and slipped his arms around her. "Isn't that bragging? Reminding everyone of how happy we are?"

"Are we not allowed to brag? I could post a picture of the ring while kissing you in the backdrop."

He blushed as his private side crept in. "As much as I would love to kiss you right now, Kenya, I think it would be over the top."

"No, this is good," she explained. She rested her hand on the mantel, fingers brushing the picture frame, and took a dozen photos from different angles. Handing Dasan the picture to put back in its rightful place, she started turning off all the lamps again. They settled back on the couch, and she flicked through photos and filters until she was satisfied. Confronted with the caption box, she chewed her bottom lip.

"How about 'Surprise'? It's certainly a big one because we haven't given our friends so much as a hint."

"Not helpful," she muttered. "How about…" She typed in her idea and angled her phone to show Dasan for his approval.

Years behind us. Forever ahead of us.

He traced her jaw with his finger, encouraging her to tilt her head up towards him. "Yes," he murmured. "That sounds perfect." He leaned forward and captured her bottom lip, nipping at it softly.

It sounded very good to her. She broke away just long enough to hit send and then turned off her phone for the rest of the night.

CHAPTER THREE

Kenya had been right when she told Dasan that there was no chance a wedding could be planned in under a year. As it was, twenty months seemed rushed. But everything got done, the day arrived, and thanks to meticulous planning, Kenya was able to relax and enjoy it without worrying too much about logistics. Even the weather had cooperated with a bright, sunny, late May day making it worthwhile to wait the extra months for a late spring wedding ceremony outdoors.

From her seat at the head table at the reception, Kenya could look out and see everyone they loved gathered in one room. That is, she could have looked up. However, she was finding it incredibly difficult to tear her eyes away from the tabletop. Dasan had moved his chair as close to hers as possible, and his left hand rested on the table between them. She had mostly covered his hand with her own left hand, making sure she could see both of their rings at once.

Somehow despite having designed the rings and picked them up over six months ago, the platinum bands were still the most shocking part of the day - seeing them on their hands. Wedding bands. They were actually married.

They had decided on having a matching design but not identical rings. Dasan's was thicker with a single diamond embedded into the band. Kenya's had a large solitaire princess cut diamond raised above the band. But both bands were made of two distinct strands, separated by a deep groove so that they looked like two identical parallel circles. They were unique, a visible reminder of each other. It was clearly working since Kenya could not stop staring.

"Kenya," he whispered against her ear. "Pay attention. You're missing how cute I was when I was five."

Kenya's sister and Dasan's mother had colluded, pooling their photos, to make an endless slideshow spanning their entire lives. Past a few baby and toddler photos, they had enough of them both together that the room had been collectively swooning for the last five minutes.

She gave Dasan a quick peck and snuggled up against him, turning her attention back to the photos. She wished she could have met him as a child, but the stream of photos was a good enough substitute. It felt like a walk through each other's lives.

"Hey," Kenya tapped Dasan's hand without taking her eyes off the screen. "Have you seen that photo before?"

"No."

"Do you remember that?"

"I don't." He turned his hand over so he could squeeze her hand, letting her know that he understood why she was asking.

The slideshow finished a minute later, and after a round of applause, Kenya went and hugged her sister, thanking her.

"Hey, there was a photo there near the end of Dasan at the lake, looks like it was the Fourth of July?"

"I know the one," her sister replied.

"Could you send me a copy of it?"

"It'll be waiting for you when you get back from your honeymoon."

CHAPTER FOUR

The couple spent their honeymoon on the Polynesian island of Bora Bora. Each day felt like paradise – the warm sand, the beautiful beaches, the all-inclusive resort, and especially the gourmet food. They spent their days relaxing, sailing, and snorkeling along the reefs. And they held each other as they watched the sunset over the ocean every night.

When the honeymoon was over, and they returned home, Kenya immediately went through their mail until she found the envelope from her sister. Then she grabbed her not-yet-unpacked carry-on bag and took out the silver picture frame she had found in a little shop in the village near where they had stayed. She gently removed the layers of tissue paper she had used for safe traveling and opened the back. She slid the picture into the frame, fastened the back, and flipped it over to admire it. In the background of the picture was a young and blurry Kenya, not more than three years old, who had been vacationing with her parents at the same lake. She was clearly walking toward Dasan, a bright and familiar smile on her face. They had definitely met that summer, but they had both been too young to remember.

Heading into the bedroom, Dasan was sitting on the floor already unpacking. She reached down and helped him stand up.

"Where do you think I should put this?" she asked.

Dasan looked at the picture of them and smiled. "I still can't believe that we met, and neither of us even remembers it."

"Me neither."

"What do you have planned for the mantel? I think this deserves a prominent place."

"I hadn't picked anything yet, so let's try it."

They had closed on their new house just a week before the wedding, with just enough time to move their things in. After the wedding, they left right away for their honeymoon. There had been little time to unpack anything, let alone worry about what items would go where. The hallways were still a minefield of boxes that Kenya knew she needed to unpack soon, or they would annoy her to no end. This seemed like a good piece to start with, making the house into their home.

She placed the picture right in the center of the mantel and then stepped back by his side to admire it. It was too small to be there on its own, but she would add wedding photos to keep it company soon enough. She rested her head on Dasan's shoulder as his arm wrapped around her waist. She reached over and took his far hand in hers.

"Do you think..."

"What's on your mind, Kenya?"

"Nothing. It's silly."

He didn't say anything. just kissed the top of her head and turned back to the photo.

"Do you think," she started again. "That if I had just seen this photo earlier, remembered this day, maybe I would have said yes sooner?"

Dasan immediately spun her around to face him. "It doesn't matter, Kenya." He said it with such conviction that she wanted to believe him.

"But look at us." She gestured to the frame, but neither of them turned to look at it.

Instead, he brushed his thumb over her cheek and drew her closer to him. "It's so obvious there. Sometimes I just feel like I wasted so much time, being too afraid to take that final step. But maybe, if I had seen this, I would have known that it was fate."

"That's not how it works, Kenya. It's not your fault. It's not your fault for not giving me an answer earlier. I didn't ask afterward either, not for two years, and I knew we were meant to be. We were both focused on finishing our law degrees. We can't change anything now, and it doesn't matter. Everything worked out in the end. We're married, Kenya. We're married now, and we'll be together tomorrow and the day after and the day after that too. Just be with me in this moment right now, alright?"

She sunk into him, with her arms around his waist and her head tucked into his shoulder. He gently rubbed circles on her back, guiding her to take deep breaths with him.

"You're right," she said, without moving.

"Occasionally."

She could hear him smirking, even if she couldn't see it.

"The universe is strange. It brought us to each other so young, and yet we didn't meet again until college."

"We didn't really miss out on all that much if you think about it. Besides, fate brought us together at exactly the right moment. I really believe that."

He was right again. But instead of telling him, she kissed him. Long and slow, savoring the forever they still had in front of them. Soon, hands were roaming. Shirts were being tossed on the ground. They made their way back to their bedroom away from the newly framed photo, knowing that things had turned out exactly how they were supposed to.

THE END

SAMARA

BLASIAN BABY BOOK BUNDLE

WRITTEN BY

JADE MOON

KIET

The name Kiet is Thai and means honorable.

SAMARA

The name Samara is Hebrew and means protected by God.

AMBW PRESS ASIAN MEN BLACK WOMEN BOOKS – VOLUME 1

CHAPTER 1

Memorial Day Weekend, 2018.

The summer night air is warm, and the clear sky is sparkling with stars - perfect for a party.

The bonfire is already blazing when Kiet arrives at Cedric and Nykia's house-warming party with three small cases of wine coolers. Nykia greets him with an energetic, gin-and-tonic powered hug, and Cedric nods toward the Jacuzzi filled with ice, a bemused smile on his face saying, *yeah, we did well here.*

"Hope you won't mind having a frequent house guest," Kiet says as Cedric nestles the glass bottles into the ice. "Are libations acceptable as room and board? This place is beautiful."

"Thanks, man. Wait until you see the rest of it," Cedric says. "Four bedrooms, three baths, two fireplaces, and full wet-bar in the basement, adjoining a spacious media room with ceiling projector and surround sound, perfect for the big game or a cozy night in."

Kiet laughs. "Are you listing it on the market already?"

Cedric admits he borrowed language from the original listing on Zillow and offers to give Kiet a tour, but Kiet declines for the moment. He is already scanning the groups of people who are scattered on the huge deck and around the fire, some planted in lawn chairs, a few dancing in the grass, many of whom he doesn't know. Finally, he sees the familiar silhouette he's looking for: Thick hourglass figure, untamed curly hair touching her shoulders, wedge-clad feet, and manicured toes: his best friend, Samara, who is with a circle of people clustered near the bonfire listening to and watching someone act out what appears to be an encounter with a bad Uber driver.

Kiet plucks two Smirnoff Ice bottles from the Jacuzzi – he'd bought the Peach Bellini for Samara – and joins them.

Samara's boyfriend, Jason, is the one telling the animated story, and Kiet is right: it's about an Uber driver.

Samara stands outside this circle a little way, her arms folded across her chest. She is wearing a fuzzy purple-colored sweater over a tight black dress. The fire dances in her brown hair. From behind, Kiet can't see the expression on her face, but he imagines she has one eyebrow cocked over her light brown eyes, an expression he knows very well which says, "I'm trying to be patient while you talk and talk and talk, but I want to *do* something else." He lowers a cooler over her shoulder to where she could easily claim it just by opening her hand.

Instead of taking the cooler, she looks back at him, her amber eyes cool despite the heat of the bonfire. Her heart-shaped lips tighten with disapproval, and she turns her face back to Jason.

Kiet sighs and withdraws the cooler, drinking deeply from his own while looking for someone else he might drink with. He has vaguely been aware that Samara has been in a strange headspace for the last month or so, but he honestly hasn't been able to find it in himself to care all that much. He's asked her once or twice if she's okay, and she's told him whatever she tells him to get him to back off, and he does because he trusts that his best friend will talk to him when the time is right. He assumes it's about Jason – a lover's spat that will either work itself out or end with Jason out the door – though Samara has never shied away from telling Kiet about all the roller coaster details of any of her relationships.

A nagging voice that he doesn't want to acknowledge whispers that maybe it's him. Maybe he did something, or said something, or was accused of something that poisoned their friendship. But he knows Samara – he knows that she would confront him if that were the case – but her silence on the subject creates an emptiness that he fills with speculation.

He makes eye contact with a woman at the far side of the bonfire circle who is not hanging on Jason's every word. Within five minutes, Kiet's extra cooler is in her hand, his arm around her waist, and he has talked her into giving him the tour of Cedric and Nykia's dream house, which of course, leads to them leaving together at the end of the night.

Kiet has spent the past few weeks drowning himself in alcohol, work, his other friends, and the occasional woman, mostly to distract himself. He has looked for Samara at the parties they used to attend together, but she either doesn't go or leaves before he arrives. He checks in with Samara multiple times every day, sending her funny memes and anecdotes about life as a Thai sous chef in an Italian restaurant with two Michelin stars. He realizes he is trying to convince himself that everything is okay between them, and as long as she doesn't stray from her typical responses (usually something sarcastic), he can believe it. Maybe that's just what their relationship has become.

A few mornings after the house-warming party, he sends her pictures of the new dish the head chef is considering adding to the menu, including cheesy baked eggs simmered in a zesty tomato sauce. Instead of texting back something encouraging, she sends a green-face emoticon, then quickly adds that she's been getting sick in the mornings. He asks if she wants him to come over – he would leave work to be with her and has untied his apron before she responds: "Thx but no. Got a lot going on rn."

That night, he arrives at his friends' bar and sees Samara at their table, backed away a little from everyone else. He studies her from across the room. Beneath her smooth, warm tan forehead and the sweep of her eyebrows, her eyes seem distant. Anyone there would think she is lost in thought, but Kiet knows her. There is a faint tightness to her lips, a barely noticeable slope to her shoulders underneath her elegant silver-sheened turtleneck, as though she carrying a secret burden. Kiet is struck by how sad, scared, and alone she looks. Surrounded by friends but not entirely with them, nor are they entirely with her.

Her drink is down to just ice, so he orders her a festive umbrella drink in a hurricane glass. He carries it over to their table and slides into the seat next to her, flourishing the personal delivery with a "Ta da!"

A range of emotions flashes across her face too quickly for him to fully process. He catches her amusement, her brief exasperation, and a bone-weariness that makes him wince from its momentarily unshielded force, before her careful composure returns. Her lips smile a little, but her chin quivers. "I can't," she says with a tiny shake of her head. "I'm trying to cut back."

"You're too young for cirrhosis of the liver, love," he says softly. "What's going on?" He is dimly aware of their friends carrying on with their conversation about hometown misbehavior, dimly aware of Cedric and Nykia, the power couple, watching without trying to watch, but he ignores them.

She holds his gaze with her sad eyes but shakes her head more firmly. "I'm heading out soon," she says, pushing the hurricane glass aside. "But thank you for thinking of me." Then, by merely turning away, she dismisses him.

Something is wrong. Which sends him on his own rollercoaster of self-doubt and confusion, hurt and loss, but most of all, concern for his best friend. He wants to put his arm around her shoulders and kiss her cheek next to her eye, where he knows she is a little ticklish, but this is not the place, and in any case, he is not the man who has any right to do this. She has a boyfriend now – Jason – and even though Jason isn't there, even though Jason might not be the most reliable or steadiest of men, Jason is the one she's chosen.

He tries to follow Nykia's story about getting busted at a high school homecoming after-party that everyone has heard before, but they are all sufficiently buzzed to laugh and chime in when Nykia gets to the big reveal: "It turns out the kid who organized the party was the police chief's son."

Samara takes this opportunity to sneak away. Kiet half-rises from his seat, but Samara gently but firmly pushes him down again. She catches the look in his deep-set eyes, unreadable to everyone but her, and the defeat she sees in his angular cheekbones sends her off the rails. She has to get out of there. She silently promises she'll tell him everything. She'll make this alright, though she doesn't know if she can keep this promise.

Samara invites him over to her house a few days later, and he knows this is it. This is where their paths are going to diverge, at least for a while. This is where she will tell him, in her own kind and serious way, that she doesn't need or want to be by his side day in and day out anymore. This is where he'll agree with her and let her go. This is where she will tell him that she's going to go to marry Jason. Or where she'll tell him that she's dropping out of her Master's program to be a model who travels the world without him. Or anything but a girl whose best friend trails around after her like a needy, identity-less puppy.

They've watched their friends go their separate ways and then come together on weekends and holidays with insincere smiles and feign interest in what the others have been doing. He figures that they'll be those people, maybe within the next few years, and it saddens him. But at the same time, he's ready for this - ready for a break from being so intertwined with another person. Just for a while. A year or two, maybe.

She opens the door and gestures for him to come inside. She already has a kettle going for tea and seats him at her kitchen table, where she has a platter of snickerdoodle cookies, homemade, still warm and fragrant. He reaches for one, a symbol of their absolute comfort with each other, though he can't deny his feeling of dread. He sees the resolute determination in her clear brown eyes and knows he must steel himself.

"No, Jason today?" he asks before taking a bite of the cookie.

She shakes her head, the spill of her bouncy hair framing her face. She has yet to sit down, partially because she's waiting for the water to boil, partially because when she does, she'll have to tell him, and in telling him, she'll have to confront her life's new reality. With trembling hands, she reaches into the cupboard for two teacups, the ones with a delicate blue pattern. They were a gift from her mother when she announced to her family that she was continuing her education. When things got tough, when she felt overwhelmed with the assignments and papers and research she had to do just to keep up with everyone else, the teacups and her own little ritual of tea were an oasis of comfort. Now that she finally feels in control of her life again, it's been shaken up so profoundly that even having tea with her best friend causes her anxiety.

She looks through her hair at Kiet, who seems outwardly calm, but she can tell by the set of his jaw and the tension of his brows that he is soaking in her anxiety, and it is feeding his own.

"Jason is no longer in the picture," she says with a faint smile that falters, never reaching her eyes. "He left. Honestly, I wanted him to leave."

There's no stopping this train now. She wants to sit across from Kiet and take his hands into her own, but she doesn't have the strength to move, even when the kettle whistles. She closes her eyes.

Kiet's inner panic is through the roof, but he tells himself that whatever she's going through – the death of a loved one may be, or maybe she really is leaving him, a thought that turns his stomach to lead after all – he can be supportive of her. He reminds himself of the day, almost a year ago, when she called him over in tears of frustration, regretting her decision to pursue a Master's degree, deciding she would drop out just as soon as the administrative office opened the next day. He'd talked her down from that cliff, and look where she is now: thriving, winning awards, turning foes in a very cut-throat environment into friends. Whatever this is, surely it can't be as bad as that.

He makes an effort to compose himself before she opens her eyes and sees any indication in his expression of the mess his heart has become. He relaxes his grip on the cookie and tells himself he is ready. He has to be ready.

"I'm pregnant," she says, and he is anything but ready.

The next month or so passes in a drunken blur.

He gets wasted that night with coworkers from the restaurant, people he doesn't know very well yet, people who don't know him very well yet either, people who don't know he has a best friend named Samara who happens to be pregnant. He doesn't think about Samara or her child even once.

He sees her at two more parties where he smiles in her general direction, and he puts his arm around her shoulders companionably. To all the world, they still look like best friends. He jokes about the odd requests made by customers at the restaurant ("Who brings a live chicken to a restaurant to be butchered?!). She describes the grueling process of gathering stacks and stacks of books for research on her thesis. It's situation normal as far as their friends are concerned.

Situation normal except for the baby, which is due in late December – "Hopefully, the little tike waits until the end of the semester," she says, exuding confidence in her ability to juggle yet another challenge. Their friends smile with admiration. Nykia, who chose her career over motherhood, even looks a little jealous.

Situation normal except for the baby daddy who split in the middle of the night. She doesn't say much about this, doesn't blame Jason, or wallow in self-pity. She doesn't want him around anyway.

Situation normal except Kiet never looks Samara in the eye.

He's out drinking with another buddy of his in mid-June when he gets a text from Samara asking how he's doing. He texts her back that he's fine and then turns his phone off.

He's been filling his time as best he can. He buys a house because it seems the adult thing to do. It's not a sprawling palace like the one Cedric and Nykia own, and it's a little bit of a fixer-upper, but it is spacious, especially since he doesn't have enough furniture to fill the rooms and can't muster the ambition to purchase more than a big-screen TV, which he doesn't watch much anyway. But he still drinks at night, every night, sometimes at the bar with friends, sometimes on the steps of his back porch watching fireflies rise and glow and dance around his yard. On his days off, he plays softball and flirts with the girls who come to watch. He even sleeps with a few of those girls, always at their place. Even when he's with them, he can't escape his numbness, how put-away he feels, as though his life has stopped despite how busy he is. He avoids any quiet time that could lead to self-reflection, drifting from one distraction to the next, and if it involves beer or tequila or vodka, all the better.

He gets another text from Samara in early July, asking if he wants to meet up. It's just before noon, and he's still hungover from the night before, hoping leftover curry will revive him, but for a second, seeing her name on the cracked screen of his phone makes him feel something for the first time in weeks.

But it isn't happiness or excitement. It's a pain and sadness and anger that he knows he cannot take out on her. He dials her number before thinking it through and inhales sharply at the sound of her saying his name.

"Hey. I got your message," he tells her quietly.

"I thought so," she answers, and he can tell her brow is probably furrowed. "I was thinking we could go get lunch this week. If you're not too busy."

He doesn't reply right away, taking the warmed up curry out of the microwave as he weighs his options. He'd like to be able to say yes. He'd like to be the bigger person and see her and make sure she's doing okay and eating and taking care of herself and her child. But he doesn't have it in him right now. He's numb most of the time, and when he isn't, he's angry. Samara is the only one to be able to get through the blanket that's muting all of his emotions, but the emotions he feels around her and about her are a mess; the chances that he'd just spew all of the garbage he's shoved down inside him onto her is too high. He may not be a great man, but he knows better than to do that to her. So he says no.

"Samara, I need some time," he tells her, voice as neutral and even as he can manage to make it.

"You need more time away from me," she says. She manages to keep her voice steady until the end when it cracks a little, and if Kiet doesn't already have an issue with self-loathing, this would have been enough to send him spiraling.

"I'll call you," he says before saying goodbye and hanging up.

He doesn't even go to the bar to get drunk that night, instead opting for whiskey straight from the bottle.

Two days later, he's helping his mother, Stella, repair a loose board on her porch. He already has the old, fractured board out and has fitted the new board in its place, driving first one nail home and then a second before moving to the middle set of joists. Stella is tending the herbs growing in pots along the edge of the porch, watering her lemongrass, and harvesting some basil and cilantro for the evening meal. His six-year-old niece, visiting for the week while her parents are on a second honeymoon, plays on a tire swing and hums a K-pop tune to herself, pigtails bouncing with enthusiasm. He loves his niece, but the humming is strangely distracting, and his head is already pounding from another hangover and the cruel brightness of the sun, and his hammering gets a little wilder, and as anyone could predict, he manages to smash the shit out of his finger.

The words that come out of his mouth and the vehemence with which he throws the hammer across the porch has both Stella and his niece looking at him like they've never laid eyes on him before. Stella's face darkens with disappointment and disapproval, but it's the look on his niece's face that breaks him.

She's scared of him.

Sweat trickles into his eyes, and he blinks it away. "Sorry, mom," he whispers.

"Go home, Kiet," she replies. "I can handle this just fine on my own."

"Okay," he agrees, wiping his hands on his jeans. He looks over toward his niece on the swing. "I'm sorry, kiddo. I don't want to scare you. Ever."

She just covers her face with her hands and shakes her entire upper body in negation.

He stumbles around the garage, wiping the sweat from his eyes with the back of his hand. He's getting into his car when he hears his mom call out to him.

"I'm going to call you later, Kiet," she says. "And you're going to be sober."

Kiet nods in response and then pulls out of the driveway.

The next morning, he calls in sick to work and looks online for a therapist who could help him get his alcohol addiction under control. He fills out the survey and is matched to Mark, a doctor specializing in depression and grief. He thinks it must be a mistake but makes an appointment anyway. Despite being a stiff, formal man who would be as comfortable in a funeral home as anywhere else, Mark is surprisingly warm and compassionate. He says that addiction is sometimes the result of an underlying problem that the addiction hides. He also tells Kiet that these therapy sessions will have a greater impact if Kiet doesn't force himself to open up and reveal all the secrets he thinks he has. "You don't have to hold yourself accountable to me," he says. "Ultimately, you are accountable to yourself. So give yourself time to pay attention to your thoughts and feelings as they bubble up from wherever they come from." It takes almost a month of weekly appointments before Kiet can relax enough to talk about more than his job, but even before then, the constant pull of alcohol loses some of its insistency.

Time passes by, with Kiet redirecting his energy from drinking and pouring it all into anything else. He spends as much time as possible working on his house, remodeling his kitchen, painting the walls in warm, inviting tones, and peeling the carpets off the hardwood floors, which he sands and stains. He buys furniture and even coasters for his dining room table, daydreaming about the succulent feasts he'll prepare for his closest friends, telling himself it'll be great, even if it's missing someone or something.

He also learns that if he plays softball sober, he can hit the ball more regularly and with more power. He tells himself that being out in the sun restores him instead of making his head throb. Oh, the wonders of being clear-headed.

He spends more time with his family, helping Stella weed her garden and mow the lawn, bringing Korean barbeque to his sister and her family. He also does his best to spend some time alone, as Mark suggests, allowing himself to really think through the mess that has been his life for the last few months. Or the last few years, really.

Everyone was constantly telling him to be mindful, be present, don't let these moments slip past you, and that was great advice, but he can see now that he likely took it to an extreme that wasn't great for who he is now. In focusing on the present, he allowed himself to ignore the past and future.

He figured he'd have a few more years to fool around, drifting after Samara, and eventually find a girl who he could maybe settle down with, drink, and party to his heart's content while he figures out what he was supposed to do with the rest of his life. In the back of his mind, the future always had Samara in it. And then she took that from him.

He's angry at himself for not being capable of being there for her right now.

He's getting there, though.

It takes longer than it should, he realizes, and the next thing he knows it's been more than two months since they've really talked. When alcohol became the center of his life, he stopped texting her on a daily basis and is finding it hard to resume the habit. He's picked up the phone a few times to text or call her, but the shame he feels about how bad a friend he's been for her, though he knows he wasn't capable of it at that moment, keeps him from pressing send.

Kiet knows the ball is in his court, that Samara is extremely unlikely to reach out to him first since he explicitly asked her not to. He's ready, and he'll text her soon. Tomorrow, maybe.

Surprise didn't begin to explain how he feels when he gets a text from Samara while he's chopping garlic at the restaurant. It's a sonogram with the caption, "It's a girl!"

This isn't even close to what he figured their first contact in months would be, but he can't help the wistful smile that creeps across his face for a few fantastic seconds. That she still wants him to have this information is precious.

Samara's going to have a daughter, a tiny human who will hopefully look exactly like her mom, who will have the determination and strength and laugh of her mother, but hopefully less hardship. A little girl who Samara will love and protect and cherish.

After his shift at the restaurant ends, he changes into a chambray shirt and black jeans, then hops back into his car without giving himself the opportunity to second guess himself. On the drive to Samara's house, he checks his motivation and finds that he's free of any resentment or anger or sadness. He's nervous, but he looks back on the last month, at the work he's done, and while he knows he's got a long road ahead, he hopes he's course corrected quick enough that he'll be able to support Samara and her kid in a way he couldn't fathom in May or June.

He knocks on her door, and it takes a little longer than he expects for her to answer, giving his doubts and self-loathing time to surface and ferment, giving him time to acknowledge his feelings and label them for what they are: ghosts of the past, irrelevant to the moment. When she finally opens her door, it's more than obvious that she's been sleeping – her hair is a slight disarray, her makeup is a little bit smudged – but worse than that, she's clearly shocked to find him on her doorstep. He feels a tiny stab of pain at this, at how estranged they've become, but he pushes the thought to the back of his mind.

"Kiet?" she asks. Her voice is sleep-filled, yes, but also completely bewildered.

"Hey." He wishes he'd brought some flowers – daisies or tulips or something summery. Now would be the time to brandish them. He smiles brightly to compensate.

"Hi."

It's been a long, long time since she's been unable to look at him when they're talking. If he'd brought flowers, they would be starting to wilt right now.

"You were asleep," he says, stating the obvious and allowing a bit of chagrin to seep into his tone.

She shrugs and tells him she was going to get up anyway to write some papers for a college assignment. Before he has a chance to raise his eyebrow in skepticism, the alarm on her phone goes off, and she holds it up as proof, with a shrug.

Samara doesn't move though. She just stays in her doorway looking past him like she's unsure of her next move, or in a completely different world. Kiet shifts on his feet, trying to come up with something to say, nervously clearing his throat, which prompts her to look up at him for a second.

"Oh. Yes. Come in." She turns and makes her way into her kitchen, immediately reaching to grab two glasses from the cupboard and filling them with water.

He takes off his sunglasses as he walks into the house, hooking them on his collar. It's then that Kiet gets to really look at her. She's wearing a short cami, and her baggy pajama pants are hanging loose and low on her hips, which means he has a perfect view of her abdomen and her small, but definitely there, baby belly. It's fascinating, and even tired and stressed and unsure as she is, she looks healthy and beautiful, and his hands are itching to reach out and learn the new circumference of her waist.

His fascination must be showing on his face because Samara looks at him in alarm and a little embarrassment and asks, "What?"

He clears his throat again. "You're doing well?" he asks.

"Yes," is all she replies, and Kiet's beginning to come to terms with this conversation being a little more difficult than what he'd imagined upon receiving that text. He should have called first.

Samara leads him into the TV room, and he can see her papers and books spread out on the glass coffee table, realizing that she really was just taking a power nap before finishing whatever she was working on. She curls into a corner of the couch and pulls her knees up to her chin, hugging her shins. He hasn't seen her this closed off, maybe ever. At least not with him. He realizes she's hiding from him, maybe trying to protect herself from him, and that breaks his heart just a little. The memory of his niece, frightened on the tire swing, is all too clear in his mind.

"You look amazing," he says, attempting to be encouraging. Trying to let her know that she doesn't need to hide from him. He sits down on the couch, but instead of plopping down and sprawling against the cushions like he normally would, he sits on the edge of the seat, facing her, doing his best to keep his posture open and respectful. He understands that he isn't exactly being welcomed with open arms, and he needs to make sure he's ready and willing to leave the second she says he needs to. Maybe even before then.

"Oh. Thanks," she replies, as she rests her head on her knees and looks across the room in the general direction of her picture window. It seems like an indication that she wants him to leave, or she wants to be somewhere else, but so far, it's a passive wish.

He finds the courage to stay. After all, the burden is on him to fix this. If it wasn't obvious before – and it was – her curt response and discomfort are screaming it at him now. He decides to go for forthright.

"I'm glad you texted me."

"That was by accident," she quickly admits, and his heart sinks a little.

"That's fair," he replies, doing his damnedest to keep the hurt out of his voice. This is on him.

He watches her close her eyes and take a few centering breaths and clenches his jaw in response. He should go. He's making her uncomfortable, and he should go. He shifts to grab his water so he can drop it off in the sink on his way out when her voice stops him.

"I obviously wanted you to know," she says with a shrug. And then for the first time in this exchange, she looks up at him and gives him a half-smile.

There she is.

"I wanted to know," he tells her.

"Then I'm glad I told you," she says with a satisfied nod. She's back to looking past him though, so he figures he really should cut this short and get to the heart of it so he can leave her to her work.

"I'm so sorry, Samara," he says, steady and sincere. He almost reaches out to take her hand but stops himself when he sees all the hurt and fear and sadness in her eyes. "I should have been here for you, especially when Jason left."

"Can I ask what happened?" she asks, and he raises an eyebrow to ask for clarification. "I know I got pregnant, and I didn't tell you for a little bit, and I know that hurt you and probably scared you. But what happened after that?"

She deserves the truth. "A lot of drinking."

"Oh," she replies in a way that indicates she has no idea what to do with that information.

He tries to clarify further. "When I left here last time, all I could think was that my best friend didn't even tell me that she was pregnant. You didn't tell me Jason left the moment he found out. I thought we were through." It sounds so stupid coming out of his mouth now, but at the time, it was like his world was ending, and his favorite person was taking it away.

She surprises him with her compassionate response and genuine understanding when she tells him, "I can see how that would hurt." She squeezes his forearm and looks him in the eye, the question obvious in her face. "Why do you think it was the end of us?"

Kiet raises his eyebrows a bit and says, "You're pregnant and having a baby, Samara." He realizes it's a stupid thing to say almost immediately because, of course, she's aware of her current state.

He can see, when she looks at him, eyes wet but glittering and fierce, that he's not the only one who has been angry.

"You left me all alone, Kiet. I tell you this huge, terrifying thing, and you just walked out my door and left," she says, voice raspy and low like she's trying to rein in her emotions.

"I wish I had a better answer for you," he says, and he sincerely does wish it. Looking back now, he can see where he had a lot of shit wrong. "I don't, though. I think maybe I thought you were abandoning me, and before you say it, I can see that that's ridiculous."

Samara makes a crack about how she's having a baby, not moving to Australia, as she retreats back into her corner of the couch, and Kiet can feel her closing herself off a little bit again.

He does his best to explain to her that he truly believed that she would be so busy with the baby that he would be forgotten. That she was starting on a new path, a new life, and he didn't have a place in it. And it had shaken him to his core, to the point where he didn't know who he was anymore. He hit rock bottom, he tells her. "And when I got there, I realized I needed to make some changes. I've been seeing a therapist – me, of all people. And it's helping me be more mindful, more aware of what I want in life."

And then something shifts, and Samara lets down her guard and lets him in again. For a few moments, he's completely overcome by how open she is being with him. She's angry and sad and scared and thrilled, and he can see all of her feelings play across her face in turn. It breaks his heart that she's so unsure of if he would want to be with her. Like there's anything else in this world he'd want to do more than that.

Oh, Samara.

"I can honestly say I don't think there's anything I want more than to stay by your side," he tells her as openly as he can.

On the drive home, all he can think is that he's not going to waste his second chance.

January 2019

Samara's messages are short and curt.

Kiet's been checking in with her each morning right around ten. Usually, the time Samara starts feeding little Amari, so he knows they are both awake, and he's not disturbing their sleep. Usually, she responds with a thumbs up or some other emoticon, but this morning, all she can give him is one letter: "K."

The uncharacteristic response has him thumbing to his favorites and hitting her name. Her distress when she answers is possibly the worst he's ever heard it, and he's pulling on his boots and jacket before he's consciously chosen to head over to her house.

He's halfway through his door before he turns back to his kitchen, grabs a grocery bag and throws containers of lunch meat, cheese, bread, and a few tomatoes into it, looks around to see if he's missing anything, grabs a tin of cookies on a whim, and then leaves his house, barely remembering to lock up.

Samara looks terrible. Her hair is a frizzy mess, her face is both blotchy and ashen, and her eyes are devoid of any emotion. She's gone into shutdown mode, something that may have worked for her a million times in the past when she gets overwhelmed, but seems to be making the baby panic.

Kiet pulls them both into a hug and frowns when it takes more than a few moments for Samara to sigh and lean in.

"She won't eat," Samara says, the utter fatigue in her voice wrenching his heart. He presses a kiss to her hair and pulls back after a bit, holding his hands out for the still screaming baby.

"Give her to me," Kiet coaxes. Samara looks so defeated when she hands the baby over that Kiet wants to scream.

The baby mewls pathetically, and the sound is like a punch to his stomach.

"Samara, why don't you go take a nice hot shower," he tells her, forcing a soothing smile onto his face. He reassures her that the baby's crying doesn't bother him, and at last, she acquiesces. He watches as Samara slowly walks out of the living room.

He doesn't have to force himself to focus on the tiny bundle. Though she's hard to ignore when she's asleep and quiet, she is impossible to disregard when she's crying her guts out, and he's amazed he managed to talk to Samara at all. Amari is wearing a little pink t-shirt that perfectly complements her cookie dough colored skin. Her head is small and covered in silky black hair. Her entire teeny weeny body easily fits in the crook of an arm. His heart breaks as he sees her lower lip quiver and big fat tears stream from her eyes. *What's wrong?* Her helpless little wails are screaming out of her itty bitty lungs. At this moment, he'd give anything to make it alright.

Kiet shifts the tiny baby, so she's in an upright position against his shoulder and starts pacing with a bouncy step, making soft shushing noises and doing his best to reassure Amari that she's safe and cared for.

"You're okay, Baby. You're going to be just fine. Cry all you need to, let it all out," he says, keeping his voice low but audible. "Life is hard, isn't it? It's so rough being out here in this big world. I don't blame you if you want to go back. Your mom is wonderful, and you probably felt safe and happy inside her. Let me tell you, though, your mom is amazing from this side, too. Maybe you can give her a break, you know? This is all new and scary for her, too." He drops kisses to her dark hair every once in a while and rubs his hand up and down her back, though she's so tiny that his hand pretty much takes up her whole back.

What he's doing seems to be working as her cries diminish and turn into these unbelievably adorable little hiccupping shudders and occasional whimpers, so he keeps walking and talking.

It's not long before Samara comes back, her hair wet against her back, and her eyes still so heavy and dark underneath, but at least she looks like she can breathe again. Samara barely looks at him as she settles into the corner of the couch, grabs a rounded pillow for nursing, and holds out her hands for Amari. He looks at her skeptically for a moment, aware that this is where she sat months ago when their relationship was uncertain, but when she tells him she needs to feed her, he hands her over.

"Do you need me to step out?" he asks, out of courtesy more than anything. He would normally be uncomfortable watching a woman nurse, but Samara's different. He chooses to ignore why she'd be different, except for acknowledging that everything is different with her.

Samara just sighs and tells him she doesn't care, so he stays and sits with them in the calm. Mother and daughter are in their own exclusive world with Kiet on the outside, but he doesn't mind as much as he thought he would. He gives them their space, fiddling with the fidget spinner Mark has given him to try out whenever he feels a compulsion to drink. He doesn't now; he just doesn't want to disturb Samara and Amari.

He looks up when he hears Samara asking Amari why she was so sad. The sadness and relief in Samara's voice has him choked up, so he offers to make her some food and sets to make her a sandwich.

They sit in the quiet as Samara and Amari eat, though he can't help but chuckle when the baby snorts and sniffles her way through her meal.

He manages to coax Samara into going to bed for a power nap once Amari is finished feeding and has fallen asleep. Soon he's alone with the baby again, though this time she's asleep in his arms and he gets to take some time just looking at her.

She's small and a little scrawny. Her ears are tiny, and her nose is a little squished. She has a serious look on her face, even in sleep, and he wonders what she dreams of. He lays her on the couch next to him, placing pillows around her, so she doesn't wriggle and roll and fall off the makeshift bed.

She wakes a few hours later with a few small cries and some flailing of her arms and legs. He picks her up and immediately smells that she needs a diaper change, so he gathers the changing pad, diapers, and wipes and forges onward. It's a challenge because he hasn't changed a lot of diapers in his life, and he accidentally ruins her sleeper, so he goes in search of something else to put her in. It's hard going, but once he gets her clean, she seems to be content to stare up at him with those intensely aware eyes as he puts on a clean diaper and gets her dressed in a light green sleeper with tiny elephants all over it.

Once she's dressed, he settles her on his lap, propping her up with a hand on her back, and watches her watching him. Her face is so serious that he can't help but smile. "How about we make a deal, sweetheart? You and I are going to be buddies. How does that sound? You want to be my buddy?" he asks with a sincerity that he doesn't understand, but the question feels important, Amari's inability to agree notwithstanding. He gently strokes his thumbs along the bridge of her nose and down the sides of her cheeks to help soothe her now that they're not moving anymore. She seems fine with the arrangement if her contented sighs are any indication. "You and I are going to do what we can for your mama, okay? We're going to have a lot of fun while your mom sleeps sometimes, and you can tell me all about how your life's been. You can tell me when you're mad or sad, okay?"

She sneezes in response and looks so startled that he grins back. "That was a big sneeze. How did such a big sneeze come out of such a little body? You're going to do amazing, big things, buddy. It's going to be so fun to watch."

He gets quiet then, and the baby stares up at him, light brown eyes so earnest, so like her mother's, like she can see right through him.

"I know your daddy isn't here to see you. If he doesn't want to, it's not your fault. He and your mom didn't know each other for very long. Your mom can be a little impulsive sometimes. I love that about her, but the results can be a little unexpected sometimes. I hope I'm enough, at least for now."

"You already are."

Samara's low, gravely, sleep-soaked voice startles him, and he can't help but feel like he got caught sharing secrets. He does his best to smile up at her and change the subject, but, of course, she's having none of it.

She squeezes herself into the space between him and the arm of the couch and lets herself sink against his side. She's obviously still so tired.

She tells him that he's been amazing, and he's just completely thrown by how grateful she sounds.

"I'm not nearly enough," he croaks out.

"You're more than enough for now," she tells him as she looks him right in the eyes. All he sees is sincerity. "We hit a bump in the road, we've hit a few bumps in the road, but the vast majority of the time I've known you, you've been my constant and no one is more supportive than you when you decide to be."

How does she do this time and time again? How does she forgive him? "You always see the best in me." He doesn't understand that, either.

"Not always. I'm not saying that the bump in the road wasn't scary, and that part of me isn't wary, but all that can fix that is time and both of us showing up for each other over and over again." She looks up at him with this weird mix of pragmatism and hope, and he's, once again, blown away by her strength and grace.

"That's the plan," he says with an easy air that belies how much he means it. It's a promise.

"I might even say that overnight babysitting is above and beyond," she says with a sheepish look.

"I'm here for you and for this baby girl for as long as you need me," he tells her, and it's the honest truth.

When Samara feeds the baby this time, he lets himself watch. He doesn't stare, but he also doesn't avert his eyes or busy himself to distract himself. Kiet lets himself sit there with them, letting himself bask in the peaceful quiet as his best friend feeds her daughter.

He watches as Samara's eyes close well before Amari falls asleep, seemingly satisfied with her meal.

He rouses Samara and encourages her to go back to bed. He doesn't have to work hard to convince her to let him stay, which tells him all he needs to know. He vows to do this more often. No one should have to do this alone all the time.

He doesn't let himself think much beyond that.

A few weeks later, Kiet shrugs into his jacket and makes sure his gloves are in his pocket before leaning over to kiss Amari on her head and Samara on her cheek in goodbye. He watches as his friend Cedric presses a firm kiss to his wife Nykia's mouth and cheek, but can't hear the low words they exchange from where he's standing.

He's hit with a strong sense of longing as he watches the uncomplicated, affectionate manner in which the couple interacts with each other. It's a girl's night in, guy's night out – Nykia's idea, which surprises Kiet since he doesn't picture the high-powered lawyer aiming to make partner at her firm as the type to be sentimental about babies. But they have a very nice house with lots of bedroom space they could fill with children; they simply chose to build their careers first.

If he were going out for a drink with anyone else, he'd probably head to his regular dive, but it's Cedric, and it seems like he wants to have a more serious conversation than is appropriate for his usual haunt, where everyone knows him, and they're more likely to get interrupted. Instead, he drives them to a low key bar that doesn't even seem to have an actual name about a mile from Samara's house.

The place isn't empty, but there are plenty of seats at the bar, and they're served their drinks quickly, a simple local lager for him, and a scotch for Cedric. Cedric tells him more about his new job as an elementary school teacher.

"It's tough being responsible for one child, let alone a whole classroom of them." Cedric shrugs with a sigh and looks to Kiet like he might have some clue.

"Amari's an easy charge compared to Samara," Kiet laughs. "Since high school, I was responsible for protecting and taking care of Samara. It was probably unfair and even a little sexist – she's so capable and was even then – but it gave me a focus and a reason to hold back when all I wanted to do some days was shake her and scream at her for her impulsiveness. Especially because those moments and impulses had nothing to do with me. She wouldn't have deserved it." He takes a drink and tries to forget that the same unchecked impulsiveness had left Samara a mother to a daughter with an absent father.

"Now you care of both of them," Cedric says as he takes a sip of his drink with eyebrows raised.

Kiet doesn't respond right away. The truth is, of course, yes. He takes care of Samara and her daughter too. He spends most of his evenings and a lot of his nights with her, and honestly wouldn't mind spending most of his days with her. He gets anxious when he hasn't seen her and Amari for more than twenty-four hours. He wonders if she's okay or if she's overwhelmed. He wonders if she's eaten well or gotten enough sleep. His arms feel empty when they're apart, and his heart feels heavy. And it's gotten to the point where taking care of her is almost a selfish endeavor. By taking care of her, of them, he's taking care of himself.

"When she lets me," he agrees after a bit.

"Because you love her," Cedric states as he stares ahead at the bottles of liquor behind the bar, giving Kiet some semblance of privacy as he takes in his words.

Because he loves her.

Kiet has loved Samara, one way or another, since they met in high school. At first, he loved to impress her, and then he loved to spend time with her, and always he loved, god he loved, to make her laugh. He has loved to see her blush, and he's loved to talk her down when she's anxious, and he's loved to tease her anytime she had a crush on another boy. He loved her steadily and constantly.

But now he loves her as a woman. As a mother. As someone who he wants to be his other half in every aspect of his life, and he looks at her, and all he wants is the best for her. He wants to make her life easier where it needs to be easier and challenge her when she needs to be pushed.

"Because I love her," he agrees on an exhale as he turns his head toward Cedric and gives him a tired smile.

"And the baby?"

Kiet can feel his smile widen when he pictures Amari. "She's the best," is what he chooses to say, but Cedric doesn't let him get away with it.

"You love her, too."

"More than I should, probably," he admits.

"Because you love her mother, or because you love her?" Cedric asks, curiosity and some concern in his eyes.

Kiet's taken aback a bit by the question. He hasn't given it much thought, and honestly, at this point, Samara and Amari go hand in hand. His love for Amari is absolutely wrapped up in his love for Samara. But if something were to happen to Samara and there was just her baby girl. He can't go down that path right now. But it leads him to some semblance of an answer.

"Both. But I absolutely love that kid," Kiet answers, and then he finishes his beer with one last gulp.

They're quiet for a moment as Kiet tamps down the panic, and Cedric sits beside him, his calm, steady energy absorbing some of Kiet's anxiety.

"You should tell her," Cedric tells Kiet, tipping his drink toward him for emphasis.

"Amari?" Kiet asks, intentionally obtuse.

Cedric just fixes him with a hard, knowing stare.

"Someday," he posits wistfully.

"Sooner is better," Cedric encourages, raising his eyebrows again, then downing the rest of his drink. "To avoid the truth because of fear, that will only lead to regret, I think."

They throw some cash on the bar and get their jackets on so they can leave. They make the short drive back to Samara's in silence.

When he walks back into Samara's house, and he sees her there with Amari cradled in her arms, Kiet is overwhelmed with the understanding that, yes, fear might lead to regret.

She looks up at him, a smile blossoming on her face. There's yearning there that he misread all this time.

"You're back," she says, and he can't deprive her anymore.

"I'm back for good," he murmurs, leaning down to kiss her gently on the lips. She smiles, sensing the promise there.

THE END

THANK YOU FOR READING

AMBW PRESS

ASIAN MEN BLACK WOMEN BOOKS

6 STORY COLLECTION

VOLUME 1

DON'T FORGET TO LEAVE A REVIEW.

PLEASE AND THANK YOU.

ABOUT AMBW PRESS

AMBW PRESS strives to publish the most beautiful and intriguing short stories, novellas, and novels featuring Asian Men and Black Women.

CONTACT:
ambwpress@yahoo.com

OTHER AMBW PRESS BOOKS

Forever Ahead of Us:

Short and Sweet Interracial Romances

The Art of Flowers: Short and Sweet Interracial

Romances

Always Back to You: A Second Chance Novelette

Dirty Divorce: AMBW Romantic Comedy

Samara: Blasian Baby Book Bundle

Takashi's Touch: AMBW Romance

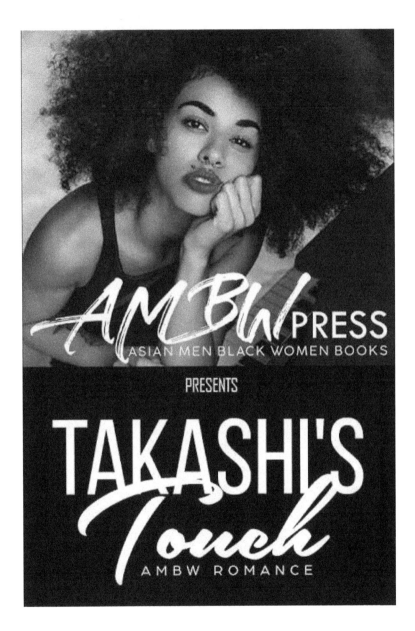

CPSIA information can be obtained
at www.ICGtesting.com
Printed in the USA
LVHW041430041119
636251LV00001B/108/P